the
DEADLINE

ALSO BY KIKI SWINSON

The Playing Dirty Series: *Playing Dirty* and *Notorious*
The Candy Shop
A Sticky Situation
The Wifey Series: *Wifey, I'm Still Wifey, Life After Wifey,*
Still Wifey Material
Wife Extraordinaire Series: *Wife Extraordinaire* and
Wife Extraordinaire Returns
Cheaper to Keep Her Series: Books 1–5
The Score Series: *The Score* and *The Mark*
Dead on Arrival
The Black Market Series: *The Black Market, The Safe*
House, Property of the State

ANTHOLOGIES
Sleeping with the Enemy (with Wahida Clark)
Heist and *Heist 2* (with De'nesha Diamond)
Lifestyles of the Rich and Shameless (with Noire)
A Gangster and a Gentleman (with De'nesha Diamond)
Most Wanted (with Nikki Turner)
Still Candy Shopping (with Amaleka McCall)
Fistful of Benjamins (with De'nesha Diamond)
Schemes and *Dirty Tricks* (with Saundra)
Bad Behavior (with Noire)

Published by Kensington Publishing Corp.

the
DEADLINE

KIKI SWINSON

Kensington Publishing Corp.
www.kensingtonbooks.com

DAFINA BOOKS are published by

Kensington Publishing Corp.
119 West 40th St.
New York, NY 10018

All Kensington Titles, Imprints, and Distributed Lines are available at special quantity discounts for bulk purchases for sales promotions, premiums, fund-raising, and educational or institutional use. Special book excerpts or customized printings can also be created to fit specific needs. For details, write or phone the office of the Kensington special sales manager: Kensington Publishing Corp., 119 West 40th St., New York, NY 10018, attn: Special Sales Department, Phone: 1-800-221-2647.

Library of Congress Card Catalogue Number: 2020935629

Dafina and the Dafina logo Reg. U.S. Pat. & TM Off.

ISBN-13: 978-1-4967-2972-9
ISBN-10: 1-4967-2972-2
First Kensington Hardcover Edition: September 2020

ISBN-13: 978-1-4967-2975-0 (ebook)
ISBN-10: 1-4967-2975-7 (ebook)

10 9 8 7 6 5 4 3 2 1

Printed in the United States of America

the DEADLINE

PROLOGUE

"*And the nominees for Outstanding Coverage of a Breaking News Story are . . .*"

I clenched my butt cheeks together and balled up my toes in my shoes so hard that they throbbed.

Kyle reached over and grabbed my hand and held it tightly.

I closed my eyes and waited to hear the results. My ears were ringing so loudly from my nerves that I didn't hear anything until cheers erupted from the crowd.

"You won, twin! They just called your name! You won," Kyle blurted loudly. He beamed with pride. It took me a few minutes to register what he was saying. He let go of my hand and helped me to my feet. My mouth hung open in a perfectly round O, and my legs were shaking so badly that my knees knocked together. I could barely catch my breath, and that instinctive right hand over my heart told the whole story.

"You have to go up there," Kyle said, urging me into the aisle so I could walk onstage and get my award.

Kyle held on to me to make sure I could balance on my heels; I guess he could feel how hard I was trembling. He walked me up onto the stage. I stood frozen for a few seconds as I turned toward the spectators. Cheers arose. My cheeks flushed and the bones in my face ached from grinning. I deserved this Emmy Award. At least that was what the loud crowd was saying with their warm cheers.

I looked over at my brother and he wore a cool grin as I slowly unfolded the paper containing my speech. I wish I could've been as cool as he was in that moment. My hands shook, but I stuck out my chest and delivered the perfect speech to accept my award. The crowd clapped and cheered again as Kyle and I walked toward the stage exit.

"Wait right there . . . hold that pose!" a photographer called out. "Smile, you're the winner," he instructed, hoisting his camera to eye level to ensure he captured the exact moment. I was blushing and sure that my face would look like a cherry in every snapshot he took.

Kyle and I posed and turned to each other on cue. We capitalized on the opportunity to take this free twin-sister-and-brother photo shoot. The photographer's flash exploded.

The bright lights sparkled in my eyes. It was truly the perfect day in my life.

"Walk slowly forward now," the photographer instructed. When Kyle and I finally made it to the end of the picture area, I was bombarded with more photographers eager to snap photos with professional and personal cameras. Noticing the paparazzi, even Kyle waved like a star. I also flashed my best debutante smile.

"Well, well, well. If it isn't the great reporter . . ." A tall man in a suit stepped into our path, clapping his hand on my shoulder. My smile faded and I bit down into my jaw.

"I didn't think you'd go through with showing up here,

all out in the public. We're all proud of you back in Nor-folk. You still got a lot of balls," he said, smiling wickedly, the bright stage lights glinting off his one gold tooth.

He turned his attention to Kyle. "You can thank your sister for everything."

I shivered.

"Ms. Mercer!" another photographer shouted, jutting his camera forward for a close-up. I twisted away from the man in the suit, happy for the distraction. Kyle and I hurried down the walkway, faking happiness so we didn't make a scene. It didn't last for long.

"Khloé! Khloé Mercer!" a male voice boomed.

My head jerked at the voice. Still smiling and faking like I wasn't about to faint from fear, I turned to my right.

"You should've stayed the fuck out of the way! You fucked with the wrong people!" the voice boomed again. The source barreled through the crowd, heading straight toward Kyle and me.

"Gun! He's got a gun!" a lady photographer screamed first.

"Oh, shit!" Kyle's eyes went round as he faced the long metal nose of the weapon. Frantically he unhooked his arm from mine and stepped in front of me. Before he could make another move, the sound of rapid-fire explosions cut through the air.

The entire place went crazy. The hired security seemed to materialize out of the walls and began running at full speed, guns drawn. Things were going crazy. Photographers, cameramen, backstage staff . . . everyone was running in a million directions. Two of the security guards were picked off, falling to the floor like knocked-over bowling pins. Screams pierced the air from every direction.

Kyle's body jerked from being hit with bullets. He was

snatched from my side in an instant. I turned and watched as my brother's arms flew up, bent at the elbow and flailing like a puppet on a string. His body crumpled like a rag doll and fell into an awkward heap on the floor, right at my feet. It was all too familiar.

There was no way I could lose my brother in this way. Not after everything. I stood frozen; my feet were seemingly rooted into the floor under me. This was just a bad dream. It wasn't real. I couldn't get enough air into my lungs to breathe.

"Kyle!" I shrieked, finally finding my voice.

"Help!" someone yelled. "Call the police! Help!" More screams erupted around us.

The sounds of people screaming and loud booms exploded around me. I coughed as the grainy, metallic grit of gunpowder settled at the back of my throat. I inched forward on the floor next to Kyle. The floor around him had pooled into a deep red pond of blood. Everything was happening so fast. I blinked my eyes to make sure this was real.

"Kyle!" I screamed so loud that my throat burned. I grabbed his shoulders and shook them, hoping for a response.

"No!" I sobbed, throwing my body on top of his. I just knew I wasn't out of danger. I knew who it was they wanted, and it was me.

More deafening booms blasted through the air.

I couldn't think as I lay on the floor. The thundering footfalls of fleeing guests left me feeling abandoned and adrift. I lay next to Kyle, listening to his labored breathing.

"Why? How did we let this happen? How did we get here?" I sobbed. "How did this all happen?"

"Hey! You've got to get out of here," a security guard huffed, pulling me up onto my feet. I was shocked to see

that I hadn't been hit. "Get out of here. Run as fast as you can and hide," he instructed. He hurled demands as fast as his lips could spew them out.

"I . . . can't . . . leave . . ."

"I'll take care of him as best I can, but it doesn't make sense for you both to die," the guard told me. "Now run!"

1

AMBITIONS

Four months earlier

I stood in the WXOT-TV evening news executive producer's office and wrung my hands. My boss, Christian Aniston, had called me into her office like there was an actual fire burning under her desk. She'd told me to sit down, but I told her I preferred to stand. I was of the mind-set that I'd rather die on my feet than live on my knees. My father had taught me that. Give me my verbal punches standing up. Everyone in the station knew about my boss's reputation. In my mind it was more ruthless than Miranda Priestly from *The Devil Wears Prada*. In fact, that character had nothing on the mean-mouthed, cruel, heartless, power-drunk, ratings-whore Christian Aniston. But I hadn't gotten this far by chance . . .

I had always worked hard all of my life. I didn't have anything given to me on a silver platter. I was a girl from the hood who was no stranger to the street life. I had grown up in a poor and eventual single-parent household in one of the most dangerous neighborhoods in the city. My father had been murdered right in front of me and my twin brother, Kyle. We were six when my dad was shot dead at my feet. I can still see how his body jerked and spun while his eyes bulged out of their sockets from the powerful shots.

I was always a daddy's girl before then. I had been standing so close to him when the man shot him, the tinny smell of his blood shot up my nose until I had been able to taste it on my tongue. To this day I remember the smell and taste every time I think about it . . .

"Daddy!" I remember emitting an earthshaking scream. Tears had burst from my eyes like a geyser. Even in the face of danger, I had thrown myself down at my father's side.

"Shut the fuck up!" the man who'd shot my father screamed, grabbing me by my hair and tossing me aside like a rag doll. I felt something crack in my back as I hit a wall inside our small town house.

"Khloé!" Kyle had called out to me. I was still on the floor when I saw Kyle charging at our father's killer. At that age Kyle was a bit smaller than I was, but his size was not indicative of his fury in that moment. Kyle growled and his small fists flew out in front of him. Swinging wildly, Kyle had tried his best to connect with any part of the man who had assaulted me and killed our father. The other man, the one with one eye, grabbed Kyle around his throat and hoisted him off his feet like he was a toy. Both men laughed, making the fine hairs on the back of my neck stand up. Kyle's little legs had pumped feverishly, like he was pedaling a bike or running an invisible race. His arms had swung like the blades of a windmill too.

The man holding Kyle by the neck had begun to squeeze

harder and harder, choking off Kyle's oxygen, until his little legs finally slowed to a halt and his arms dropped at his sides. The color had faded from his face and his eyes rolled up until all I could see were the whites. Fear had put a stronghold on me, and my stomach muscles had clenched so hard I wanted to faint, but I scrambled to my feet instead, and ran into the man holding my brother.

"Let him go!" I had hollered, and bulldozed into the man's legs. I opened my mouth as wide as I could and chomped down on his inner thigh, the only thing I had been tall enough to reach back then. I was like an attack dog. I sank my teeth into the man's leg and used every bit of strength in my little jaws to latch on like a steel-jaw trap.

"Agh!" the killer screamed. "You little bitch! Get off of me!"

With that, the one-eyed man had no choice but to let go of Kyle's limp body and they both dropped to the floor. I finally released my jaw and freed him. I watched in horror as Kyle jackknifed onto his side, wheezing and coughing until the color started returning to his face. But because of the bite, the other man turned his attention to me. Suddenly I felt the cold kiss of a pistol against my temple.

"Shoot the little bitch!" the one-eyed man had growled, still writhing on the floor. I closed my eyes, and my bladder released all over my feet as I sobbed.

My mother bursting in with the cops was what had saved our lives.

After my father's murder, we moved a lot. My mother couldn't cope and she started using drugs heavy. She could no longer care for me and Kyle in the way she had before my father's death. The state stepped in and took us. That forced my mother to finally go to rehab.

Unfortunately, there would be several stints of drug

rehab before she stopped relapsing, and while she struggled, Kyle and I lived in many different foster homes. If that shit did nothing else, it had toughened me up. Tragedy has a way of making clear what you want for your life. I knew then that being poor and dealing with the dangers of living in the hood wasn't the life for me, so I fought to stay a straight-A student all through my schooling.

I completed graduate school and earned my master's degree in journalism. I wasn't going to just stop there. I had big dreams of being an on-air news anchor, so I'd taken this job as a news research aide here at ABB affiliate WXOT-TV in Norfolk, Virginia.

I was working my ass off too. Unlike all of the other little flunkies around here, I was one of the only ones bringing in interesting stories. I had done all sorts of shit to get good stories. One time I took a job as a bartender in a strip club to blow the lid off a story about someone who was setting up and robbing strippers. I was there the night the damn robbers decided they were going to step up their game and not just rob the strippers when they left at night, but the whole damn club. Just my luck. I had been behind the bar with my back turned when I heard the first scream a short distance from where the bar was located. The noise had caused me to almost drop the bottle I was holding, and before I could turn around, another echo of screams reverberated through my ears.

Silver, one of the newest strippers at the club, belted out another guttural scream that threatened to burst my eardrums. She had been the first one to notice the dudes filing in with their guns out in front of them like they needed them for direction. I had whirled around on the balls of my feet just in time to come face-to-face with the barrel of a black pistol.

"Where's the fucking money, bitch? And don't try nothing funny," one of the masked men had snarled. All I could see was the fire flashing in his eyes. I had actually seen the pupils of his eyes and they were devil red. I knew then that nothing but sheer evil resided in that man. Silver would not stop screaming.

"Shut her the fuck up or I'ma blast both of y'all bitches!" the masked man growled at me. I turned on her so damn quick.

"Shh," I warned her harshly. "Be quiet or we are dead."

Silver quickly clamped her left hand over her mouth to stifle her own screams. I could see that her body was trembling like a leaf in a wild storm.

My head was swimming with fear. I didn't think going undercover for a story would have ended up like this. It made me ask myself, how far was I willing to sell my soul for the perfect story?

"Y'all bitches better get down right now before I lay y'all down. This ain't no bullshit!" the masked gun-waving robber had barked. It was traumatic, to say the least. To have his gun leveled at my face had put me back to my childhood, for sure. I couldn't help but think that there must've been a reason God kept putting me in these situations.

"Please, please, I . . . I . . . can't die . . . please," Silver had started begging.

"Just do what he says and be quiet," I instructed Silver. Just then, two more strippers, Blaze and Billie, were herded out of the dressing room in the back into the main club area where we were. The other robbers put them down on the floor facedown. Both were begging and pleading for their lives too. They were crying, but I just couldn't bring myself to cry. Maybe I was numb. Maybe I was ready to die. When the robber holding Silver and me had turned, it gave me a few seconds to sneak my cell phone and hit the record button. I hadn't done all of this *not* to get the story. If I was going to die, at least there would be something left behind.

"Bitch, I said where is the money?" the robber boomed after only getting about six hundred dollars from behind the bar. I had almost jumped out of my skin thinking he had seen me sneak the phone. My hands were shaking. I swallowed hard as my eyes darted around wildly. There were three more gunmen in my immediate sights. All sorts of things had run through my head, but my thoughts were quickly interrupted when I noticed another gunman dragging the club owner, Sly, into the main club area too. Sly was bleeding from his head. I knew then he had been hit with a gun.

"Please don't kill me," Sly begged. He was begging and crying harder than some of the women in the club. The Big Bad Wolf that he had pretended to be had surely changed into a blubbering bitch in that instant.

With sweat beads dancing down the sides of my face, I moved forward apprehensively to the register to see if there was any more money inside to offer the gun-wielding thieves.

"There's not a lot of money in the register," I said, raising my hands in surrender to let the masked gunmen know I wasn't going to resist. "But in the back . . . there's a safe. Sly can get you inside. He's the only one who knows how, so if you hurt him . . . you'll end up with nothing." I locked eyes with Sly. He looked relieved, upset, hurt, all in one glance. I didn't care. I wanted to get out of there alive, especially because my ass shouldn't have been there in the first place. *All for a story. All for a story,* I kept chanting in my head.

"I want every dime! Every dollar, you fucking bitch!" the second assailant growled through the black material of his mask, while two more had yanked Sly up from the floor and started dragging him to the back.

"If this nigga try anything funny, y'all are going to find his brains all over that office," the masked man had said. His words had taken me back to seeing my father shot dead, and a shot of heat spread throughout my body. For the first time since they had busted into the club, I had felt sheer and pure fear grip me tightly around the throat. It had been so bad, it made me gag.

"Take the bartender too. I think she know more than she's saying," the biggest of the robbers had said, pointing his gun in my direction. I shook my head no, but it was too late. They'd snatched me up and dragged me to the back with Sly. All the way I was praying Sly didn't try to front on them. I knew he was scared, but I also knew he was an asshole.

"I . . . I . . . don't know . . . um . . . anything," I had pleaded. I was desperate because I wanted him to believe me.

"Bitch, nobody asked you. You're my insurance policy, just in case your fake-ass gangster boss here act up. Now shut up!" he boomed. His words had reverberated through my skull so hard, I felt like it had shaken my brain. I swallowed hard. I was pushed forward. I stumbled toward the back office. My insides churned so fast that I just knew I'd throw up. Once we were in the back office, they tossed Sly down in front of the safe. He got to his knees and I could see that his hands were shaking badly; he could barely twist the knob for the combination lock. Who the fuck still has a dial combination lock and not one with a keypad? But I had quickly learned from the short time I'd gone undercover at the club that Sly was a cheap bastard. He treated the strippers like pure shit too. All of this had probably been his karma, but I couldn't understand why the universe would involve the rest of us if it was paying Sly's ass back.

"Don't fuck around, you punk-ass nigga! Don't play like you can't open the shit. I ain't got no problem spilling your brains," the main gunman had ordered, swiping his gun across the back of Sly's head.

Sly winced and frantically fumbled with the ancient combination dial again. I finally heard a loud clicking sound. I breathed out a sigh of relief.

"Move," the gunman had demanded, and pushed Sly down onto his back. I heard Sly's head hit the floor so hard even I felt it.

"Fill this shit up," he called out to the others. They all filed in with black garbage bags that they'd pulled out of their jackets. The other two robbers went about filling their bags. I couldn't believe how much money Sly had in that safe. It didn't even look big enough.

When they were done, Silver, Blaze, and Billie were all brought into the office. The robbers made us all sit together with our backs against one another.

"Stay sitting like this until we are out of here, or else I will spray all y'all," the tallest and meanest of the gunmen had commanded. It was almost over, and just like everything else in my life, nothing could just go smoothly.

"You niggas ain't going to . . ." Sly never got a chance to finish what he was saying. Before he could utter another word, a loud crunch sounded through the room. The metal of a gun had connected with his skull. Sly didn't stand a chance. The impact from the blow of the gun knocked Sly out like a light. His body slumped to the left and blood leaked out of his head like a faucet. It was the last act of violence before the robbers fled.

When it was all said and done, I had the exclusive, but I was also traumatized as hell. When I brought the story in,

Christian was all impressed back then. She had bragged on me in front of all of the other assistants and junior reporters. I could see them green with envy. It had happened several more times too, when I'd had to get down and dirty to get a story.

At first, I was rewarded at the studio for how gritty and real and up close my stories were. They didn't ever ask me if I was all right after nearly losing my life a couple of times for a good story. I didn't care either. I was in their good graces. Within a year and a half, I was promoted to an off-air journalist, and in no time was dubbed the most valued junior segment producer.

Granted, most of my stories up until now had been about robberies and prostitution rings and some car larcenies, and in my opinion those were interesting. But those types of stories weren't where I wanted to be in the end. I had big dreams and the biggest was that I would get a seat at the six o'clock on-air news anchor desk. I knew I had my work cut out for me, and if you asked me, I'd say I had been doing what I needed to do to get there.

Still, even after risking life and limb for stories, here I stood in Christian's office with my mind reeling backward in a million directions and her staring me down with a look of disgust like I was a pile of dirty laundry.

"You sure you want to stand there looking all goofy?" Christian asked without cracking a smile. You would've thought she was joking, talking to me like that, but there was nothing funny about her tone.

"Yes, I'll stand," I said, barely above a whisper. She had that effect on me. Around Christian, I felt like the kid that got called out in front of everyone for saying the dog had eaten her homework. Getting called in by Christian was nerve-racking, to say the least.

"Listen, Khloé, you've done some decent work thus far. I won't take that away from you, but if you expect to earn a seat at the news desk, you're going to have to act like a real journalist and step up your game. You've gotten to the point where petty theft and hood rat robberies just aren't going to cut it anymore," Christian said, constantly licking her dry lips like she always did when she was acting like a straight passive-aggressive bitch. I wanted so badly to tell her to kiss my ass and that I had been going above and beyond to bring in quality stories, but she was my boss and I *did* want a permanent seat at the desk, so I just shut up and let her have her moment.

"I'm working on it, Christian. I just don't know what else to do. I get out there and get involved, you know that from my past stories," I said, biting down into my jaw. This bitch shrugged like she didn't care.

"And your point is?" she shot back in a sarcastic manner.

That comment made my blood pressure rise. "We are the local news, so we pretty much have to go by what is happening in the area to predict the types of stories we will have. I can't just make stuff up," I said, trying my best to keep my voice level. I mean, what did she want me to do . . . kill someone for a story? I almost died twice getting stories from the streets!

"You've been saying the same thing for a month now. It's up to you. I would think you would want to make sure you secure a spot here at WXOT-TV, right?" she pointed out.

"Wha . . . what do you mean?" I asked, my voice crackling with fear.

"I mean that nothing is guaranteed . . . not even the job you have right now. If you don't pull your weight around here, there are thousands of other hungry young reporters out there that would love to be in your shoes," Christian shot back without one ounce of empathy. She was a cold bitch, and she didn't care who knew it.

"Are you saying my job is at risk?" I asked, my heart racing at an alarming rate.

"Well, you said it, I didn't," she said sarcastically. "What I am saying is you need to stop standing here looking like a silly kid and get your ass out there and get me a story worth this station's time and money," she finished up.

I felt angry tears burning at the backs of my eyes, but there was no way I could cry in front of Christian. That would have definitely been career suicide. I turned on my heels fast and started for her office door.

"Khloé," Christian called at my back.

I stopped walking, but I didn't turn around. I wasn't going to give her the satisfaction of knowing she'd rattled me to the core.

"Just know that if you can't do it, then you can pack up your belongings and leave the building so I can get some-one who really wants to give me a great story," she said, speaking to my back. "It's business . . . never personal," she continued.

I swallowed hard, the cusswords I had ready for her ass tumbling back down my throat like a handful of hard mar-bles. Without saying another word, I left her office in a fury.

Everyone in the whole studio must've heard Christian chewing me out because as soon as I closed her door be-hind me, everyone was staring. I rolled my eyes at every single one of those ass-kissing clowns. And how dare that bitch Christian threaten to take away my job! She was going overboard now. I mean, why all the fucking pres-sure?

I'd done a lot to get some of the stories I'd brought in so far. For the past year I had always been first on the scene to store robberies, home invasions, some carjackings, and a few snatch-and-grab street robberies. I guess those weren't good enough. Not good enough to make it to the prime-time news desk, for sure.

Christian wanted me to get an exclusive. A scandal. Something so big, the whole world would find out from us. A story that would make the news station move into the number one spot again. All of the pressure to blow up the ratings was on my back. I guess when I didn't tell her to kiss my ass that meant I had accepted the challenge.

Nothing I had in mind as I walked to my car was good enough. I was going to have to get out in the streets and find some juicy stories. But damn . . . Christian had me almost wanting to create stories to keep my job.

2

STREET TIES

It had been three days since my meeting with Christian and my story prospects so far had been nothing more than an old lady getting her purse snatched and a hit-and-run driver that caused a three-car pile-up on Virginia Beach Boulevard. I'd gotten pictures of the fire that resulted from the accident, but unless someone's charred remains were in the photos, I knew Christian would snub them.

I was at the end of my rope. I couldn't think anymore. I decided I needed to go see my mother. She always knew how to comfort me, whether it was with her good cooking or sound advice. I didn't always get to have that mother-daughter relationship with her, so we were kind of making up for lost time over these past few years that she'd been drug free.

I shook my head to rid it of the memories of the past. I had worked hard to forgive my mother for the things we'd gone through. I had moved on from the hurt and anger, but on days like this, when I was super stressed-out, those memories still came back. I tried not to hold it against her, but sometimes indirectly I blamed her whenever I was hurting or stressed. I guess you could say it was just a bad cycle of thoughts.

I put my car in park, breathed out the breath I'd been holding when I was remembering the bad times, and put on a smile. I needed my mother right now. No sense in dwelling in the past. I rushed up to the door and knocked. Too full of energy, I tried the knob before she could get to the door and it was open.

"Hey, baby girl," my mother sang as soon as I crossed the doorway into the house. She rushed over with stretched-out arms for a hug. My mother still looked good for her age. She was curvaceous like me, and although I'd taken after my father with my hazel eyes and sandy brown hair, I had my mother's shape. We both stood five-five and had Coke-bottle shapes—flat stomachs, small waists, and nice round hips. My mother was gorgeous back in her day. The drugs had taken a bit of a toll on her looks, but not as bad as some other addicts I'd seen in my lifetime. I was just glad she'd made it out on the other side.

"Hey, Mama!" I returned the greeting and walked into her embrace. I closed my eyes for a few seconds, appreciating the love. She smelled like warm cocoa butter as usual. That was a secret she'd passed down—cocoa butter to keep the skin looking young. The smell made me feel nostalgic and loved.

"Okay . . . what's wrong? You know I can sense it as soon as I touch you," my mother said, her tone serious as she pulled away from me so she could look at me. I could see the concern in her eyes. "You and Kyle have that twin bond and can feel each other's pain, but I have that special bond with both of y'all. I know every time something is not right with either one of you." She continued looking me over hard, as if she would be able to tell what was bothering me by sight.

I sighed loudly. My mother had been saying that same thing all of our lives. She always told us that her bond and her ability to feel what we felt when we were happy, sad, hurting, or in distress was how she knew we were in danger the day my father was murdered. That was how she'd busted in with the cops and saved us in the nick of time. I sighed again and flopped down on her couch. I leaned my head back and stared up at the ceiling in silence for a few minutes. I had to gather my thoughts on how I was going to talk about how I was feeling. I was stuck between looking weak and helpless (something I hated to portray), or just being honest so I could get shit off my chest.

"C'mon, I'm waiting to hear what is going on," my mother pressed, not giving up. "And you know I am not going to stop, so you might as well just tell me. I don't take no for an answer when it comes to my children being in distress."

I sat back up and shook my head. There was no fighting my mother on this, because I would be fighting a losing battle with her.

"It's this job," I groaned, swiping my hands over my face. I was exhausted just bringing up the topic.

"I thought you loved the job," my mother questioned, sitting next to me on the couch.

"I do . . . I mean, I did . . . It's just that . . ." I didn't even know what I was trying to say. My brain was muddled with the pressures of nabbing the perfect breaking-news story. All I could think about was Christian's threats and her nasty ways. It was a lot to process and to talk about all at once. I was silently wishing I'd chosen to go to Starbucks, instead of coming to see my mother. I wasn't a talker like this. I'd failed at therapy for years because of it. I was a suffer-in-silence person who just made shit happen in my life. This was difficult. "I don't even know where to start. It's just a lot," I finally said, dreading to reiterate what had gone on back at the office today.

"Calm down and talk to me, baby girl," my mother comforted, stroking my hair. It was a little weird whenever she had these big displays of affection. I was still getting used to our new and building relationship. Sometimes my mother overcompensated because of her guilt from the past, but this was one time I was appreciative of her efforts.

I blew out a windstorm of breath and eased the tension in my neck and shoulders. I turned slightly so I was facing my mother. I guess I wanted her to see the distress in my eyes. I guess I wanted her to know I needed her, but was too set in my ways to ask for her comfort.

"Okay, how can I explain it so that you understand how bad it is?" I asked the question, but wasn't expecting an answer.

"The best way to say it is, my boss, Christian, is a bitch. That's first," I spat with a bit more venom than my mother was probably used to hearing from one of her kids.

"Watch your language," she said immediately. Then she softened a bit. "Go ahead, I give you a pass because you seem very stressed-out."

I shook my head a little. *This lady forgets I am grown. I am twenty-seven years old and can cuss whenever I like.* I didn't say that, though. *Once a mother, always a mother.*

"Anyway, Christian, the Devil in disguise, has loaded me down with the task of getting a breaking-news story that will blow our ratings through the roof. She wants some exclusive that no other station in the area or in the nation, for that matter, will have first. She has made it clear that it is the only way I will ever accomplish my dream of becoming an on-air prime time news anchor. She even threatened my current job, which, you know, with all of these student loans from grad school, I cannot afford to lose," I relayed to my mother with tinges of angst underlying my words. Honestly, saying it all made me feel like someone had lifted a one-thousand-pound weight from my chest. I let out another long breath and felt slightly better. I guess my mother was right about how beneficial speaking to her about my problem was for me.

"Hmm, what kind of story does she want?" my mother asked, rubbing her chin as if she could help me. "I mean, news is news, right? You can only report on whatever you know to be happening. Sounds like she is expecting a miracle in this little area," my mother continued.

"She didn't say exactly what type of story, which is another thing all together. She just wants something so hot it will make the whole world want to know and watch our news station. My entire life and livelihood are hinging on me bringing in something that would blow her socks off. As if I could just come up with something off the top of my head like a damn fairy godmother or something," I said. I was so disgusted by Christian's never-satisfied ass. I could've just screamed and pulled all of my edges out by hand.

Just then, Kyle started fumbling with the locks to get into the house. My mother and I both turned our attention to the door as he used his key to come in. After he closed the door behind himself, he bopped toward us with the street swagger that he swore made him so manly. He was funny. I smirked because as hard as Kyle played, I knew he was a loving brother. We looked like the male and female version of one another, but we were vastly different in most ways.

Where I had always been strongly independent, Kyle was more needy and dependent. He was still living with my mother at our age. Sometimes it annoyed me, especially when I had to pay my bills at my place. I would sometimes be left with fifty bucks to get me through until the next paycheck, while I knew Kyle was here mooching and living for free. Every dime of his money was his to spend, which was why he could afford a fancy car and lots of high-end clothes. Yeah, it sometimes annoyed me to know he was living the good life, with no real worries, but other times I felt better that if I couldn't really look out for him, because I was off on my own, then him being here with my mother meant that she could.

"Aye, twin," Kyle sang, in the smooth, street way he spoke. His hazel-colored, cat-shaped eyes were low, so I knew he had just blazed some weed. That was another habit he'd picked up as we grew up—smoking weed. My mother got up right away. She hated to see Kyle after he was drinking or getting high off weed. I guess it was kind of a trigger for her. She said she would go make me some food and left the room with quickness. It was odd to witness her scurrying away like that, but I was too busy greeting my brother to think too much of it.

"Hey, twin," I replied, standing up to give him a hug. Sure enough, Kyle smelled like he'd just burned an entire field of marijuana plants around him. I didn't scold him this time. I was glad to see him. My brother and I were closer than close. He was my other half, even when I had boyfriends. Nobody really came in between my brother and me. I'd dropped many dudes over conflicts with Kyle. If they couldn't accept my close relationship with my twin brother, then they couldn't accept me or be with me. Kyle and I were bonded from the womb, and that was no exaggeration. When Kyle was sick, I was sick, and vice versa.

The only thing opposite about us was the path we took in life. I chose to go to school and go "the lame route" (as Kyle called it), and he chose to go the street route and be in the mix, like both of our parents were in their heyday. Kyle was into a little bit of everything and made his living off the land . . . literally. Kyle was like the middleman to everyone in the streets. If you wanted something, you could always go to him. It could be as simple as information, or as complicated as a whole houseful of furniture. If you asked for it, Kyle could get it. Kyle was the literal hustle man of the neighborhood and he had his ear to the streets about everything. Nothing got past my brother. Nothing at all. I always thought that could be a good and a bad thing. I was always worried about him out there doing nefarious shit to get money. The world was a crazy-ass place.

"What's wrong with you?" Kyle asked, immediately sensing something with me. I still thought that shit was amazing, and it had been.

"Damn, you too," I said, chuckling. "Mama just did the same damn thing when she hugged me. That's so crazy. Y'all really act like that bond thing is that serious."

"C'mon, twin. You know better. You know I know shit when you feeling down and out or hurting," he replied, one eyebrow raised like I should already know this. "I can feel it all up in your body and see it all up in your face. You're stressed about something. It better not be no nigga stressing you. I will tighten somebody up over you, twin."

"It is definitely not a nigga stressing me, boy. And, really, what's going on with me is actually not that big of a deal when it all boils down. My boss giving me shit, that's all," I said, not really wanting to elaborate all that much, all over again.

"Who is he? You know I don't play that. He might be

the boss at that job, but I'm the boss in real life," Kyle said, cracking his knuckles for emphasis and his face going serious.

I laughed a bit and pushed him on the arm playfully. "First of all, it is not a *he,* it's a *she.* And I don't need you to beat anyone up like when we were kids. She's just giving me a hard time about my story content. She's pressuring me for a big story. She's always putting the pinch on me for bigger and bigger stories. No matter what I bring in, no matter how good it is, she is never satisfied. She wants some kind of scandalous shit that she feels will earn me the spot on TV that I've been working for. She is even hurling threats around that if I don't come up with something soon, she will be forced to let me go . . . blah, blah, blah . . . You know how white people with a little bit of power act . . . like they're the master and you're the slave," I explained.

"Damn, she sound like a real bitch," Kyle replied. "I know you be out there getting busy with them stories too. Your ass even be going undercover and all that. I remember that robbery at that strip club, while you was under in there trying to get a good story. And what about the time you was faking like a prostitute to find out who was snatching them prostitutes off the street down there?" Kyle recounted. He shook his head in disgust. "What more the bitch want? She want you to sell your soul to the Devil or some shit?"

I shook my head and agreed with what he was saying. I'd been going hard from the day I started working at the station. "I don't know. She keeps using the word 'scandal,' 'scandal,' 'scandal.' She doesn't want your run-of-the-mill robbery or missing person. She wants something bigger and better. I'm just at a loss, that's all I know," I said, even though I knew that I wasn't going to get any real feedback from him. He wasn't big on giving advice. He was more of a listener than anything. But for some odd reason he seemed engaged and concerned. I watched him as he rubbed his chin, just like my mother always did. He looked like he was thinking, and I was shocked.

"Shit, I know plenty of scandals you can report on," he finally said, taking his hair pick from his pocket, sticking it into his neat Afro, and picking his hair as he spoke.

"I've already tried these petty-crime stories. You just said you remember the robbery I almost died trying to report on and the prostitution thing I went undercover for. That type of street shit won't fly anymore, twin. She doesn't want any more of those," I said, lowering my eyes to the floor. "She wants something earth-shattering, I guess. She wants me to be standing over a dead body, or chasing down the killer, or something that will shake up the world," I said, gesturing with my arms spread wide.

"Don't discount the shit I know, sis. My shit ain't all petty-crime stories," Kyle said like he was a tiny bit offended by my comment. "You think everything I got my hands in is in the hood?" he asked, chuckling. "Think again. They don't call me worldwide K.Y. for nothing, you dig? I can rub elbows with the best of them . . . from track-suits to tuxedos, feel me? I know some real scandalous shit involving people you'd never think about being involved."

I tilted my head to the side. "What are you talking about?" I asked, intrigued now. Maybe he was onto something that I needed to know.

"See, see, now you want to know what I'm talking about," he taunted.

"Just tell me," I shot back; my patience had worn thin.

"How would your bitch of a boss feel about a scandal involving the possible future mayor of Norfolk being involved in all kinds of illegal shit?" he asked, rubbing his hands together like he was cooking something up in his mind. "How would that be for an earth-shattering story?"

I moved to the edge of my seat; my eyebrows arched on

my face. "What do you mean 'the possible future mayor of Norfolk'? Like, a candidate that is running?"

"I mean, what if the number one candidate for mayor, Anton Barker, who is currently the defense attorney for some of the most ruthless-ass, drug-dealing killers walking the streets, is running for mayor of Norfolk so he can let all that illegal shit go down and keep getting paid by the criminal clients he's been defending all of these years. What if I tell you that behind that suit and tie and white-tooth smile, Barker is a two-faced motherfucker pretending to be a politician, but is the biggest criminal walking?" Kyle replied, a wicked little grin spreading over his lips.

"Stop playing with my emotions, Kyle," I grumbled at first. "Are you making this shit up as you go along? This sounds like something from a TV show or movie."

"You ain't got no faith in me? You ain't learn over all the years we been alive that I don't play around all of the time?" he asked, shaking his head at me.

"Wait . . . are you being serious? Or are you just talking shit?" I asked, my heart speeding up with excitement. "Because I'm in a real tight situation here with my boss and I don't have time to play around. That story sounds like exactly what that bitch Christian is looking for."

"I'm so serious, twin. I can get you that story, but we gotta be careful, though. That nigga Barker ain't no joke. All of us street niggas know better than to get too close. Only pretty women can get close to him. He got a thing for bad chicks, if you know what I mean. But on the same token, he goes through a lot of shit to hide and protect himself, feel me? He plans on becoming mayor in a few months. That is, unless you break this story and bust up the election, but just know if you do that, you might have to have a lot of protection around you afterward," Kyle said, his tone getting serious. "Be sure you're ready to live like that for a while. It would be like being in Witness Protection or some shit. Always looking back over your shoulders."

I didn't care about my brother's warnings. All I heard was "ratings, ratings, ratings," which equaled to me being on that 6:00 p.m. news anchor desk.

"How? How can I get in on this?" I asked, jumping to my feet. Within seconds I was pacing, which is what I did whenever my mind started racing. I could've walked a hole into my mother's carpet as much as I was moving. I had so many thoughts rotating around my head. I couldn't figure out if I was coming or going.

"It may take selling your soul, just like your boss expects," Kyle answered, but then he laughed. "Shit, we both going to sell our souls, for that matter. I would be dragging you into something you might not be ready for. You may have to get inside his campaign office or even push up on the nigga to get closer. Like I said, he has people working for him already and he rubs elbows with all the major players in the game here in Norfolk. I don't know if you're ready. He also has cops and judges and the like on his payroll. Let's put it this way . . . Barker's friends are all killers in suits. So I don't know if I even want you involved, now that I think about it."

"Stop playing," I told him seriously. "You can't tell me about this and then pull back now. I definitely don't have time for any games. This is my story. I can feel it, Kyle."

I didn't have time to be strung along. I needed to know if I was going to have something I could go back and tell Christian.

"Pump your breaks, sis. I'm not playing at all. Stick with me and I'll take you to the first of many places to build up the story. You just have to be careful with the information until you have it all together, because once you blow the whistle on this, we might all have to run for cover. Barker is dead set—and I do mean *dead set*—on becoming the future mayor. He has defended the biggest dealers in our area. And he is not only powerful, he is ruthless and don't give a fuck about nothing. He is the Devil in a suit," Kyle warned.

"I don't know about y'all doing this," my mother said, her voice shaky. She'd returned to the living room with a plate of food for me, but I hadn't even heard her come back. I was too busy being keyed into what Kyle and I were discussing about the story line.

"I don't think anything is worth selling your soul to the Devil for. This man sounds like someone you need to steer clear of," my mother went on. My first thought was that she had some nerve. I had watched her sell her soul to the drug devil a few times. She couldn't judge me at all. I kept those bad thoughts in my head, though.

I flopped back down on the couch and sat quiet for a few seconds. Christian's voice rang in my head: *"Nothing is guaranteed . . . not even the job you have right now. If you don't pull your weight around here, there are thousands of other hungry young reporters out there that would love to be in your shoes."*

That was enough. I wanted whatever Kyle was going to give me. I wanted my job. I wasn't listening to anyone other than my inner voice, which was telling me this was going to be my big break.

My mother set the plate of liver, onions, white rice, and gravy in front of me, but all of a sudden I wasn't hungry. Kyle switched on the TV. "Watch this . . . I bet the nigga is on TV smiling and kissing babies right now as we speak about his ass," Kyle said, flipping through channels until he came to our rival station's news.

I sat up straight and watched. My heart was beating so

fast, I felt the movement behind my eyes. Sure enough, as fate would have it, there he was, the now-infamous Anton Barker, standing behind the reporter waving and smiling like the quintessential politician. I couldn't front, the man was fine. He had a nice build, which was not too skinny, but not too muscular. His hair was salt-and-pepper, and so was the goatee that ringed his smooth cocoa-colored skin. His suit was clearly custom-made and expensive. It looked like he spared no expense on his upkeep and appearance. I liked it. I liked it a lot. I watched the television screen and stared as my rival station nemesis, Jay Jones, walked over with her goofy smile and microphone. Even she made googly eyes at Barker as she jockeyed for a good position and camera angle.

"We are here at the biggest mayoral campaign event for top candidate Anton Barker since he announced his bid for mayor of Norfolk. The people seem to love him. This crowd has eclipsed every other candidate in the race. It seems that the people of all sections of the city love Mr. Barker. We have reported before how it seems Barker has a stronghold on all classes of voters."

I watched, glued to the television, as Jay Jones pushed her microphone past all of the other reporters and wedged her way in, to get a word with Barker.

"Mr. Barker, sir. Tell us how you manage to appeal to so many people. We've seen you defend what some would call the dregs of society, but now here you are, being loved by everyone," Jay Jones said, her microphone directly in front of Barker's mouth. He straightened the lapels on his jacket, flashed a beautiful, gleaming white, straight-toothed smile, and spoke eloquently.

"Well, let's just say I am a man of the people . . . all people. I come from humble beginnings and worked my way through law school. It wasn't easy, so I understand the plight of every man, woman, and child in Norfolk. From the rich to the poor, I've been around them all. I will continue to serve the people," Anton Barker answered, never letting his smile drop from his face.

I was flabbergasted by his words. He was smooth, gorgeous, and now I knew that he was also a liar. I shook my head, side to side, and squinted at the television. It took a special kind of person to lie so smoothly. I was convinced in those few minutes of watching Anton Barker that he could sell salt to a slug or talk someone right into a brown paper bag. From what Kyle had just said, the beautiful specimen of a man I was looking at on TV might as well have been a serial killer, based on the crimes he had defended and the ones he had also committed. It could only take a psychopath to switch identities like that. And what better type of story to report on than one about a two-faced, double-crossing, double-life–living psychopath that was running for the top office in our city?

I stood up. I was too uncomfortable to stay seated at that point. A bunch of theories and story preps ran through my mind at once.

"What you thinking, twin?" Kyle asked me, noticing my face. He suspected that I was onto something.

"I have to have this story. This is going to make my career, and there is nothing else I want to do now," I said, kind of in a trance. "He has got to be stopped if everything you've said is true."

I could actually envision myself breaking the story to Christian. She'd jump up and hug me so hard that I wouldn't be able to breathe. This is the kind of story that would put her past work to shame. They would be begging me to be on that news desk. I might even steal Christian's job out from under her, like she did to Lucy.

"I know I have no place in telling you-all what to do. We've lost some years and you both are grown, but this all just doesn't sit right with me. I feel danger down in my gut and bones—danger for everyone involved, not just you, Khloé," my mother said, looking like she was on the verge of tears.

But when I became a reporter/journalist, I knew what I was signing up for when I applied for the job. I couldn't afford to let someone else get an exclusive story on him. I'd be in the unemployment line the following day. Now what I can do for my mother was assure her that everything would be fine.

"I promise you, I will be careful, Mama, but if there is a scandal going on in Norfolk, I am going to be the one to break it. I don't care if I do have to sell my soul," I said, meaning every word I had uttered. I was ready to go after the infamous Anton Barker full steam ahead. *Six p.m. news desk, here I come,* I cheered in my head. I could picture myself now, getting a whole new wardrobe and hiring a glam squad because I would have to be on point.

3

DOWN AND DIRTY

"A'ight, Khloé, you see that cop right there?" Kyle pointed through his windshield as we sat in his car hidden across from the Norfolk Second Patrol Division station house. My legs swung in and out nervously. Kyle had called me at home. He told me to hurry up and get dressed; he had to show me something related to my story.

"Which one? There are a few," I replied, craning my neck to see whom he was talking about. "There's one that's not in uniform. You mean him?" I squinted to see.

"Yup, that one. He is a detective. He's a dirty detective in every sense of the word. He works directly for your boy, Barker, the possible future mayor, and all of his clients, but he pretends he's out here solving murders. More like out here committing them and then solving them like he's the best," Kyle told me.

"Are you serious?" I asked. I know Kyle was getting tired of me asking that, but some things were just so unbelievable.

"Man, I know of at least six murders commissioned by

people associated with Barker and his clients and cleaned up by this cat in front of us. He plants evidence, he gets rid of evidence, and I've heard sometimes he carries out the murders himself too. The reason I said to follow him is, I think after a while, he will lead us right to Barker's hideouts."

I sat staring out of the windshield in astonishment at what Kyle was saying. How could someone who'd sworn an oath to protect and serve be doing what Kyle was saying. I guess I was being naïve, since that shit happens all over the United States every day.

"That is crazy. He looks so straightlaced and clean-cut," I replied, my mouth still hanging open a little bit as I watched the smooth detective chop it up with a few uniform cops before heading to his car.

"Appearances can be deceiving, for sure. He's the only person with his hands a little dirty that our friend will take visits from. He's the insider/outsider, if that makes sense. Barker is smart. He tries to keep his hands clean, even though him and his clients run all this shit around here. Every single nickel and dime sold in Norfolk, Barker gets a cut. He's like the Pablo Escobar of this city," Kyle explained.

I was struck silent as I listened and watched the clean-cut and dapper detective get into a darkly tinted black car.

"So, how can I get something newsworthy if we can't get next to Barker?" I asked, still a bit shocked at what Kyle was really telling me.

"We going to follow him right now, but we got to be careful. You know he's police, so his countersurveillance skills is top-notch," Kyle explained as he cranked up the car. As soon as the engine started, so did my nerves. I had to bite down hard to keep my teeth from chattering. Biting my nails was the next best thing, so that's what I did.

"This is the time of day he makes some stops at the secret stash spots to pay for the re-ups and collect money sometimes. I heard from one of my street connections that they about to blow the lid on a dude they suspect of turning on one of Barker's biggest clients' spots. Which, in turn, means, it fucks with Barker's cut and all the dudes on payroll cuts. My connect said he knows once the detective finds out dude was being a traitor, he is going to take care of the situation right then and there, since the possible future mayor and his clients only trust him to deal with it," Kyle told me.

Kyle slowly and carefully pulled out behind the black car. My heart throttled up in my chest, because everything Kyle was saying sounded extremely dangerous. But that news-desk job was still calling my name. I imagined the shocked look on Christian's face when I got this whole story solid, and that was enough to keep me moving closer toward danger. I told myself to sit back and go along for the ride, because everyone knew that in the journalism business, there was never any reward without a little risk.

It seemed like we had driven forever when Kyle finally stopped the car. I moved my head around, peering out of all of the car windows trying to figure out just where the hell we were at. No lie, it looked like we were transported in time and place. We were in some backwoods part of Virginia, and the property that sat in front of us looked like an old abandoned farm or plantation. There was a big, dilapidated, and haunted-looking plantation-style house to the left, and almost in the way back of the property was an old shack. It looked like if one bad wind came through, it would collapse.

"What the hell?" I said, mouth hanging open a little bit.

"I told you, these dudes are very careful with their shit. Barker actually purchased this old plantation so that he could have a place for his most dangerous clients to conduct their business. We are not dealing with dummies here, twin. Everything they all do is well planned and thought out," Kyle said. As he spoke, I took in eyefuls of the area. We were so far from any civilization that if anyone screamed out, there was not a soul in the world that would hear him. That thought gave me a bit of pause too. If we needed help out here, not a soul in the world would hear us either.

We couldn't pull the car right up to the secret property that the detective had driven to, so we stopped down a road, where Kyle parked between some trees. It had taken a little maneuvering to get the car situated where no one could see it. Just the thought of what we were doing made adrenaline pump through me.

"What now?" I asked. "We can't see anything from way back here."

"Relax," Kyle replied, digging in his center console. He pulled out a damn blunt. I watched him like he was losing his mind as he prepared his lighter to spark up his blunt.

"I'ma smoke this, calm my nerves, and then we going to get out and sneak around back, once the outside coast is clear," he told me.

"Really, Kyle!" I shouted a little too loudly. He fumbled with his blunt and lighter, and every little movement he made was on my nerves. I rolled my eyes at him in disgust. "Do you really think it's a good idea to be getting high right now? Don't you think doing something as dangerous as this takes a clear mind?" I asked, seriously disturbed. It always annoyed me to see him smoke weed or drink until he was drunk. At a time like this, when I felt like he needed to be fully sober just in case anything went left, I was especially upset.

"Listen, twin, if you want me to get you these exclusive pieces to build your story . . . you going to have to shut up and let me work. Go with the flow. There is always a method to my madness, and if anyone ain't going to steer you wrong, it's me," Kyle chided, then lifted his blunt and took a long drag off of it. He inhaled deeply and blew the smoke in my direction.

I fanned the air with my hand and crinkled up my face. *Shit, maybe Kyle is right.* I was feeling so wrecked in the nerves that for a second I felt like I needed to smoke some weed. That thought quickly faded, though. I had never taken a drug in my life. I hadn't even experimented with any because of the devastation drugs had done to my family. My father had gotten killed over selling drugs; and after seeing my mother addicted to heroin and crack and battle her way back from the edge of death, I felt there was no way I would ever do drugs. I sometimes wondered why Kyle even smoked or sold drugs. Like, what in his consciousness could allow him to even want to be within an inch of any type of drug was beyond me. He had been right there when everything happened to us. Just like me, Kyle had lived through the worst of times due to drugs. I turned my head and stared out of the side window, waiting on him, and that was a mistake. The sight of my mother overdosing flooded back into my mind, fast and furious, like the rushing waters of the Louisiana levees breaking during Hurricane Katrina. There was no stopping that memory. I closed my eyes . . .

I'd been hiding by the wall in our new apartment and watched yet another dude that my mother had brought home coax her into taking something.

"Listen, I ain't never sent you wrong before. Live a little. I don't have to bend your arm to make you feel good. You know you want to get high like before. You been chasing this shit since the very first time . . . You know what it is," the dude said to my mother, and then grabbed her arm and pulled her to our table.

I came around the wall a little bit so I could see better. My little heart was pumping hard, and I remember curling my hands into fists as I watched.

The man watched my mother. His eyes were wide, and he was breathing hard, like watching my mother readying herself to take the drugs had excited him. Who got that excited over drugs? For a quick moment I wondered if my mother would finally get some sense and refuse the man's peer pressure.

"Linda, baby . . . go ahead. I promise, you going to feel good as hell after this hit," the man had urged, grinning slyly. From where I stood, I could see sweat beads on his forehead; every time he moved, they made him look shiny and evil. My mother had crinkled her face as if she wasn't sure. I had watched her try to be happy after my father's murder and she'd had a lot of seedy friends come through our place at the time, but I could tell in that moment she wasn't sure that being with this man was worth trying something that might get her addicted. As young as I was, I could see the strain of apprehension in my mother's face.

"This is some new shit. Trust me, it's the A-grade shit that you'll love. I got it from my boy Drago. He always got that good shit. I'll always be able to get my hands on this shit after today. Wait until you get a taste," the man had said, urging my mother on and on.

I bit down into my jaw and swayed a bit on my little legs. I weighed my options in that moment: If I rushed out and screamed, my mother wouldn't take the drugs, but she also might be very upset and beat my ass. She had become really unpredictable at the time. Some days she was our loving mother that we recognized, and other days not so much. My mother was getting into drugs heavy. It had gone beyond her just smoking a weed joint, like she had done when my father was alive and they'd party. My mother was walking the line into heavy stuff that she'd always preached against to Kyle and me.

"I don't know about this. This is something different you talking now," my mother had said, still not sure. "You know I like you, but I do this for fun. I can't afford to get in too deep. Addiction is not what I need right now," she said.

The man grunted and sighed loudly. When he moved around the room to face my mother, I looked at him really good in the light. He was gorilla ugly, and he already looked like a strung-out fiend to me. I squinted my eyes as he dumped a small mountain of the drug onto the back of his hand. The man stood over six feet tall and his arms bulged out of the sleeves of his T-shirt. I would've been no match for that monster. He towered over my mother, who was even slimmer than before from not eating a lot since the murder. My mother's skin was still pretty, but her eyes were sad and sunken now. Before she'd had the deepest, darkest brown eyes, with thick black eyelashes, that always caught people's attention. But as I watched, I noticed that her eyes were ringed with dark circles and sad, very sad. Her thick, long hair was always in a ratty ponytail and she hadn't let it down to flow since before my father's death.

I was eight, but I was smart beyond my years. Where other kids might've missed the stark contrast in their mother's appearance and her overall deterioration in everything, I had definitely noticed. That night I felt my heart break a million times as I stood there and watched. It wasn't that I hated my mother, but I was devastated that she'd let these outside forces interrupt her life, to reach this terrible point. She looked so weak to me. I had felt a flash of embarrassment and a stab of hurt. I kept watching her and thinking that if she continued using drugs, she wasn't going to be so beautiful for long, nor was she going to be our mother for long.

"Stop being scared, Linda. I'm not going to ask you again. You ain't going to get addicted, if that's what you're worried about," the man had shot back. "Now either you down or not? I can go find someone else to have a good time with." With that, he placed his nose on top of the mound of white powder on his hand and inhaled like a high-powered vacuum cleaner. When he was finished, there was absolutely nothing left on his hand. Then he dumped out another mound of the stuff and pushed it toward my mother. I was screaming *"NO!"* in my head, and to keep from screaming it out loud, I clamped both of my little hands over my mouth. I watched my mother finally give in and she held one side of her nose and inhaled with the open side. My stomach had cramped up as I watched.

"Ugh," my mother had grunted as her legs buckled a little bit. I thought she would fall, but she just stumbled around, all the while keeping her balance. "Shit!" she had shouted, and then she started laughing, as though the man had told a joke. My mother started doing some crazy dance. She had jumped around like a fool. It was crazy to watch. After a few seconds, I guess, she remembered that the man was still there. She circled him like she was doing some mating dance. He laughed too.

"I told you this was that good shit. You ain't want to believe me, right?" the man had said, laughing at my mother, but clearly satisfied he had her.

When he dumped out more drugs, the hairs on my skin stood up. I felt my entire body tense up; somewhere in my little brain I sensed danger. Call it our bond or instinct, but in that moment I knew something bad would happen. I had told myself I needed to run in and save her, but I froze. I couldn't move, as if my feet had grown roots into the carpet. The man had a small pile of the drugs ready for my mother again.

"Don't be scared, sexy. Just take it in and forget all of your troubles. This shit here works wonders," the man had said, smiling wickedly at my mother. I had seen the Devil himself in that moment. My mother was laughing, but I knew better. It wasn't happy laughter. I didn't have a good gut feeling about it, but I couldn't move. I watched in horror as my mother bent down and inhaled like she had no cares in the world.

"Yeah, baby!" The man grinned, urging my mother on. "This is what is going to take you away from all of your troubles. This is your new daddy. I'm telling you, sexy . . . you will never be the same after this shit. Just like my man Drago said, we can use half the amount and get doubly as high. This is *that* premium shit, baby. You going to love me forever for showing you this shit here," the man was saying as my mother took yet another large inhale of the drug. She was giggling the whole time, like she was giddy as hell.

"Let's go. You're going to experience more happiness than you've ever known. Get your mind right and have a good time. You can't walk around worrying about shit all of the time. Life is for living, and this shit here is for taking!" The man kept up his pep talk.

"Yes! Life is for living while you have it," my mother sang.

I flared my nostrils and breathed in. I was holding my breath. My head felt swimmy and I wanted to scream. I felt buried alive in my own body, and, boy, this was a horrible feeling.

My mother sniffed again. This time she reacted like someone had slammed a hammer into her chest. I had watched in horror as she stumbled backward. She immediately threw her hand up over her nose, and tears leaked out of her eyes. She held on to the sides of her head as if she were trying to stop some kind of pain or slow her mind. The man was laughing hysterically at my mother's reaction.

"Oh, shit. What the fuck?" my mother grumbled as she shook her head. Within seconds she was moving as if she were floating. Then, out of nowhere, she was back to happy and giddy. She stumbled around, trying to find a seat. Finally she slumped down into one of the kitchen chairs.

"I see light . . . a lot of light. All colors," my mother had slurred, her head moving around slowly. Her lips curled into a smile, but it wasn't a happy smile.

I was seeing that my mother had no control over her own body parts. One minute she would barely be able to stand, and the next she'd leap up for a few seconds, singing and dancing and jumping around. She'd flop back down into the chair and stop moving for a while. She looked like she couldn't move, even if she wanted. My mother hung on to the chair for dear life, because every few seconds she looked like she thought she'd fall. Her mouth was moving, but she wasn't saying anything.

Seeing her like that had truly broken my heart. My eyes had filled with tears and I contemplated going to wake up

Kyle. I knew he'd probably rush in and save my mother. But again, for some reason I was stuck, unable to move. I blamed myself silently, yet I still couldn't stop watching.

My mother waved her hand at the man as he dumped another small mound onto his hand. In my head I was screaming, *"Mommy, don't do it!"* But my mouth wouldn't move.

"I love it, I love it, I *loooovve* it," my mother sang. I couldn't believe her. But I watched as she deeply inhaled yet another little mountain of drugs through her nose. Her reaction was instantaneous.

"Agh!" my mother belted out. She bent over at the waist for a few seconds. That's how powerful whatever she sniffed was. Then she stumbled around, took another small amount of the drugs, and placed it up against her nostrils again. She opened her arms wide, like she was about to try to fly. She started spinning around and around, looking like a child playing the get-dizzy game. My heart was pounding as though I had run miles and miles at top speed.

I watched as my mother spun around in front of me. Sweat poured down the sides of my mother's face. Finally she had worn herself down until her body finally collapsed to the floor. My mouth opened, but I couldn't scream. I suddenly felt like I was suspended in the air.

"Help me," my mother gasped. "I can't see. The light . . . the light is clouding my eyes," she continued, squeezing her eyes shut. "Help me!" she screamed out.

The next thing I saw was some unknown force moving her body like she was being electrocuted. I suddenly felt a cold breeze whipping around me. I remember shivering, but I was unable to cover myself with my hands.

"Ay! C'mon, get up," the man shouted at my mother, using his foot to kick at her body as it jerked violently.

I didn't know if she was dying or what, but suddenly I was able to move and I rushed out of my hiding spot. I was plastered to her side, screaming, "Mama! Mama! What's wrong?" I felt like throwing up, but nothing came up. She was not inside her body, which was painfully clear now. Now I knew what people meant when they said, when you die, the soul leaves.

From my view my mother was dead in that moment. She was sprawled haphazardly on the floor. Her beautiful legs were splayed in an awkward position that looked like it hurt really bad. "Mama! Wake up!" I hollered. When her body stopped jerking, she resembled one of my broken Barbie dolls. As for me, I felt the pee leaving my bladder from my nerves.

"Mama!" I screeched. She had gone still and was lying flat on her back. Her mouth hung open, her eyes were wide, staring straight up at nothing, and her hair lay around her like a death shroud.

"Get up, Mama! Get up!" I was screaming, but nothing happened. I was stuck on that floor, looking at my mother, but she lay on the floor stiff. I wouldn't leave her side to go get Kyle. I was praying he would wake up from my screams. I couldn't breathe, and that throbbing in my heart had already stopped. I couldn't help my mother or myself. I was powerless and I couldn't wake her. I looked around, and the bastard that got her like this was nowhere to be found. I wondered if he had a conscience and was regretting giving my mother the drugs.

It was useless to keep screaming. We no longer had a phone in our house. I didn't know if I was going to be stuck there forever, or if someone would eventually find us. I definitely wasn't leaving her. The feeling of powerlessness was one that I had never experienced before and the one that I couldn't understand then and probably would never be able to speak about again.

"Mama, you can't go. You can't go," I cried, placing my

head on her chest. After that, I just remembered a flurry of activity and suddenly Kyle was there. The last thing I remember thinking was, if she lives, I will make her proud, and I will never, ever use drugs in my life.

Kyle suddenly blew out some more smoke and snapped me out of that nightmarish memory of watching my mother overdose. I shrugged off the thoughts about him and his drugs. I figured, to each his own. And if after what we went through, he still didn't care about what drugs could do to his life, who was I to tell him? I'd done all of that when we were teenagers. The counselors we went to as kids and teens had said both of us would have our own coping mechanisms as we grew up. If nothing else they said was true, that statement definitely was. Kyle and I had chosen different ways to cope with all of the tragedy in our lives. My coping came through pouring myself into school and becoming utterly obsessed with being a successful journalist and on-air reporter. Kyle's way of dealing was getting involved in any- and everything that was against what society said was right.

Kyle woke up daily to find ways to buck any system he perceived was holding him back. He often got high and went on for hours about government conspiracies and "the man," as he called it. I never really knew who this "man" that was holding us all down was supposed to be, so most times I just nodded and agreed. It was common in the hood to hear dudes that refused to work or make their lives better through school say stuff like "the white man" or "the man" or "the government" was holding them back. Although, if I had to put a face on the so-called oppressive "man," he would definitely look like my boss, Christian Aniston!

I still loved my brother more than anything, though. He

was my everything. I would die for him, and I'm sure he would die for me too. Our bond was as strong as steel.

"A'ight, twin. I'm ready," Kyle announced, stubbing out his blunt and breaking up my thoughts. "This shit is now or never. And just know the things I do for you, including this crazy-ass shit, it all out of love."

I inhaled deeply and exhaled a shaky, nervous breath. "I'm ready too," I said tentatively. "And I love you just the same, brother."

"Make sure you have your phone on silent and no flash on your camera. I bet there will be a lot to take pictures of . . . Shit, you may get lucky and see the man himself," Kyle told me.

"You mean Barker?" I asked.

Kyle chuckled a bit. "That's a reach. That nigga is like a ghost in the game. Just fix your phone so you don't get us killed. Not right now at least." Kyle laughed again, but I didn't find anything funny. My brain was on alert from that moment on.

I fumbled with my cell phone to make sure everything was the way Kyle said it should be. I cued up the phone camera to make sure the screen was there when I was ready for it. Sweat started pouring down my back and across my forehead. I could feel the nerve in my left eye jumping. That's what always happened when I was nervous, in distress, or just plain scared out of my fucking mind. I didn't know what we were about to walk into, but I said a silent prayer that we would make it back out. Kyle started out of the door, but I grabbed his arm and stopped him.

"Wait . . . what's the guy's name? The detective," I asked.

"In the streets we know him as Redds, but his real name is Marlon Keith . . . so I guess at the station they call him

Detective Keith," Kyle replied. He shook his head. "The dude really does live a double life. You'll see. I can show you better than I can tell you. That clean-cut, dapper, happy cop you saw ain't going to be what you see now . . . I'm sure about that."

I shook my head in amazement. This was crazy. There was already an unbelievable story forming in my head. I could even see myself reporting on it from the live desk. My insides tingled from the thought.

"C'mon, we only have a small bit of time," Kyle said with a bit of urgency.

"Okay," I said, grabbing for my door handle too. I stopped for a second again.

"Kyle."

He turned and looked at me with an awkward frown.

"Just know that I love you, no matter what. And thanks for always looking out," I said sincerely.

He straightened up his face and smiled. "We don't have time to waste today, twin. We need to be on our square," he replied like a schoolteacher. He was a stickler for time and staying on our A-game. We needed to be on high alert.

Kyle and I exited the car in the bushes. I followed his lead as he ducked down and practically crawled toward the back of the little shack. We stayed low and my knees were burning. I was out of shape. That little bit of crab walking had done me in and I was huffing and puffing, trying to catch my breath by the time we both made it to our destination. I swallowed hard and fought to catch my breath. Kyle did a couple of hand motions that let me know we were at the place that Redds, or, better yet, Detective Keith, had gone into. Kyle signaled for me to crouch so I could look into the cracks in the wood. The slits seemed to have been made to perfectly fit my eyes. I looked through and watched and listened. I was amazed all over again. This was like some crime-movie shit playing out. I could hear so clearly, it scared me. *If I could hear them, could they hear me creeping around outside?* I thought. Still, I couldn't stop watching and listening.

There was a bunch of men standing around. Some were black and some Hispanic. It was like two sides about to go to war or something. Each side flanked their apparent leader, and each side held their guns in plain sight.

"Let's do this," Detective Keith said, like he wanted to get to the business at hand. He had changed into a black leather jacket and black jeans. A far cry from his suit and tie. He didn't look like he was there to make small talk. Also, a far cry from the smiling and chatting we saw him doing outside the police station. A guy dressed in a black hoodie and black jeans turned toward another guy dressed the same; the only thing distinguishing them apart was their different-colored footwear. In unison the clones walked a few paces and retrieved two black duffel bags from the spare tire well in the back of the vehicle they had come in. It wouldn't have been believable except I was watching it go down.

Even through the little slits in the wood, I could see the strain on their faces as they lugged the bags over. A Hispanic man with a head full of dark, curly hair, and dressed similarly to Detective Keith, walked over, flanked by two of his men. His men weren't wearing all black; in fact, I thought they were dressed pretty bright for this kind of transaction to be going down. I could tell these guys were on different sides because they held guns at their waists like they were on the ready for anything that might pop off. They all watched as Detective Keith's workers unzipped the bags to reveal crisp new stacks of cash bound with thick red rubber bands. I moved my eyes from the cracks in the wood and looked over at Kyle, who was peeking through another crack. I made a gesture to him that said, *Gotdamn, do you see that money?* He widened his eyes and shook his head, as if to say, *Hell yeah, I see that shit!*

Voices coming from inside made me put my eye back to the hole. I listened closely, fully enthralled and nervous.

"The first bag is for what we received last night on the first shipment. The second is the first half of what is owed for the missing shipment," Detective Keith said smoothly, like he was an old-school drug dealer and not actually a cop.

My heart fluttered under my rib cage like a moth trapped in a jar. So far, I'd seen enough to build the most scandalous story ever. I could feel the cogs and wheels of my mind turning with ideas on how to report on this.

"Check it," the Hispanic man said, nodding and handing the bags off to his partners. The two men meticulously lifted each stack of cash, flicking through them as if they were decks of cards. As fast as they flipped, I could tell they were still being meticulous about the count.

"All here," one of the Hispanic man's henchmen said. When they were done counting the money and secured the bags in their vehicle, the Hispanic man stepped closer to the crooked detective.

Even from my position outside and looking in, I could feel the palpable tension inside. I hurried up and got my phone out. I put the camera up to another tiny slit and tried to record and watch what was happening at the same time. It was risky, I know, but I had to at least get a little bit of footage so that Christian would believe it. I mean, if I were in her shoes and a junior reporter came in with this story, I might not believe the shit either.

"There's something else. I have one more point of business to discuss," the Hispanic man said, looking around the room and then back at Detective Keith.

I raised my eyebrows in nervous anticipation of what was to come. A hot feeling came over me, which told me something was about to go down. When your gut tells you something, it is usually correct. Anything was possible in this type of business. At least that is what Kyle always told me.

"I know this will be hard to hear, but I have to do as I was instructed," the Hispanic man said, sounding as if he was stalling.

I could see Detective Keith shift his weight from one foot to the next, listening intently.

"Get to it," he grumbled, impatiently looking at his watch.

"My boss wanted me to let you know that there is a traitor in your midst," the Hispanic man finally relayed, his words dropping like a grenade in an open field. It even made my breath catch in my throat. I moved my eye for a split second to compose myself before I blew my cover.

"What the fuck are you talking about?" Detective Keith exploded, placing his left hand on his waistband. "Don't come in here making accusations you're not ready to defend. Me and my boss don't take kindly to that shit," he snarled.

The Hispanic man's men moved in like ready soldiers. Detective Keith's men followed his lead, with their hands on their weapons as well. It looked like a gang-turf war about to go down.

"Listen, I'm not here to fight," the Hispanic man said, putting his hands up to ward his guys off. He addressed Detective Keith directly, agitation lacing his words as he bit down into his jaw. "My boss asked me to deliver this as proof to our claims. We don't ever make allegations that we can't support. You should know better than that. We are in the same business, and sometimes shit like this can't be avoided."

I sucked in my breath as I watched the Hispanic man reach inside his pocket and take out a package. It was a fairly large envelope. All of Detective Keith's men shifted in the distance behind him, the metal of their weapons clicking and cocking. Detective Keith took a few steps back, not sure what the next move would be. The Hispanic man and his men did the same, holding their guns at the high ready. Detective Keith tore the envelope open; it was like what was inside was going to determine everyone's fate. I could see that his hands were shaking. Everyone's eyes were glued on him, including Kyle's and mine. It was like time had stood still. The anticipation was buzzing in the air. I thought I could actually hear it. I didn't even want to blink my eyes, for fear I'd miss something. Detective Keith finally got a look at what was inside. From where I stood and peeked, I could see what looked like pictures in his hand, but I wasn't sure. Suddenly I could see the dirty detective's shoulders slump and he inhaled deeply. The scene inside that remote shack was so intense; even I found myself swallowing the fear that had formed into a ball in my throat.

What the fuck is it they have? My mind raced. I needed answers. And I needed them quick.

"Proof," the Hispanic man said calmly, folding his hands in front of him like a praying priest, as he watched Detective Keith hesitantly sift through the contents of the package.

"This is bullshit! They playing games right now! You don't have to look at shit they got to offer," one of the detective's workers suddenly shouted from somewhere to his left. The guy came rushing over and tried to use his body to knock the contents out of the detective's hand. "We came here to pay for the shipment. Period. All this extra shit is not needed!" the same worker shouted; his tone was laced with panic.

Kyle looked over at me and gestured as if to say, *I told you so!*

"Why is your man here so nervous?" the Hispanic man asked Detective Keith, gesturing to the loud worker, who clearly didn't want whatever was in the envelope to be revealed.

Watching it, I had to agree with what the man had said; that worker seemed guilty and nervous about what might be found out. It was a clear indicator of guilt. Detective Keith stepped around the Hispanic man toward his group of workers. I felt an uneasy tightness in my chest as I watched it all play out. My mouth hung open slightly as I watched the detective review whatever he had been handed one more time.

"Damn," Detective Keith said breathlessly, shaking his head. If I didn't know any better, I would've sworn I could see the heat rising from his toes up to his face, because his cheeks turned beet red. I bit down into the side of my cheek as I watched him flip from one incriminating photograph to the next. I looked over at Kyle. My nostrils flared as I tried to keep my breathing under control.

"Where'd you get these?" Detective Keith asked the Hispanic man through his teeth. "Where the fuck did you get these!" the detective boomed, not giving the man a chance to answer.

"A mole we have working on the street turned the information over to my boss. Our people followed up, and this is what we found out. We saved your life today with this information, Redds," the Hispanic man said gravely. "If you cannot believe what I am telling you, we have more proof that this is true," he continued, raising his hand to one of his men.

One of the man's henchmen, who looked like a heavyweight boxer, disappeared. Kyle and I both ducked down when we realized he had come outside in the front of the shack.

"Shit," I huffed, my back against the wall of the house and my chest heaving. Kyle put his fingers up to his lips to shush me and then he got back up and peeked. He signaled for me to do the same. While doing so, I watched as the boxer-looking dude dragged another man into the shack. The guy was quivering; he was blindfolded and gagged too.

"What the fuck is going on, man?" Detective Keith's guilty-acting flunky growled, his voice unsteady. It looked like everyone was on edge. I could hear their angry and confused murmurs. Their heads were swiveling around, trying to figure out what was happening. It was one heartbeat from sheer pandemonium.

"Let's go," the guilty dude barked. "I'm not feeling this shit right here." The others mumbled their agreement.

"Shut the fuck up!" Detective Keith commanded; his voice sounding more authoritative than he'd been since I'd started watching them. He still clutched the pictures against his chest; they were in his grasp as if something would change.

The tall, dark-haired black dude had been dragged from the Hispanic man's vehicle. I sucked in my breath at the man's poor condition. His hands were bound tightly in front of him and he was being pushed toward Detective

Keith and his men on weak, shaky, bruised legs. He only wore his boxers and a bloodied T-shirt. From the looks of it, it seemed someone had worked him over pretty damn good. He looked terrible.

"Start talking!" the Hispanic man barked after he pulled the gag down from his mouth, shoving the beaten man forward. I couldn't stop looking at the man's battered face— half-shut eyes, his clearly broken nose, and his protruding split upper lip. The abused man refused to speak.

The Hispanic man snapped his fingers at his goons. One of them rushed over, grabbed the tattered victim by his neck and hoisted him off his feet. He squeezed the man's throat until he was gagging. I held my breath and hoped they didn't kill him right in front of my eyes. I didn't know if I could stand to watch that, story or not.

"Put him down," the Hispanic man demanded, right before they would've caused the battered man to go unconscious. "Now . . . tell him what you know!"

"The guy . . . he told me . . . he told me . . ." The battered man coughed and garbled out his words, barely able to formulate each syllable on his lips. He could barely speak through his swollen mouth, and the blood made it even worse. He would gurgle blood every other word. I really had to strain my ears to hear him.

"Louder!" the Hispanic man barked, kicking the man in his ribs so hard that I winced and moved so hard that Kyle whipped his head around and shot me a look as if to ask if I was damn crazy.

"The guy . . . your guy . . . he . . . he . . . wanted to kill you. He . . . he . . . made a deal with us. He told me about this meeting today. He . . . he . . . tried to set you up to be killed and robbed here today. He would get paid, once we took the money and the shipment, and he told us how to go after your boss later," the man said through his busted lips, blood dripping from his mouth onto the floor.

My mind screamed as his words hit home. I knew right then that shit was about to go bad . . . very bad. I looked over at Kyle and he shook his head. We probably should've been getting out of there, just in case a crazy shoot-out went down, but we were both glued.

"What the fuck is he talking about? I want to know what's going on right now! This is a setup! This nigga gotta be lying!" the guilty dude screamed, getting in the Hispanic man's face.

Detective Keith was screaming for an explanation. The Hispanic was trying to convince him that what he was offering was the truth. The guys were behind the both of them, yelling that they were ready to leave, that these Spanish motherfuckers could not be trusted. It was all too much. It was a garble of loud voices and chaos.

"Quiet!" Detective Keith finally shouted, causing everyone to pause midsentence.

"Believe what you see in those pictures, Redds. My boss is never wrong, and he never lies," the Hispanic man said calmly. "Count this as a gift. We don't give a fuck about too many people we do business with, but we figured in this case you would want to know about this."

My body was engulfed in heat now. Something ticked in my brain, like a bomb was about to explode. It was about to go down. I positioned my phone so I could get some footage.

"This is bullshit!" the guilty dude shouted. "You going to believe these spic motherfuckers? They just trying to make trouble!"

"Shut the fuck up!" Detective Keith finally exploded, tossing the pictures onto the floor at the guilty dude's feet. "Everybody just shut the fuck up for a minute!"

Everyone seemed to look down at the pictures at the same time. It was as if time had stood still. I squinted through the slats, but I couldn't make out the images. I could only imagine how bad they were. The hum and buzz of the groans coming from everyone in the room sounded like a swarm of angry bees about to attack.

"Satisfied?" Detective Keith huffed, kicking the pictures toward them all. The guilty dude quickly fell silent. "Are your own fucking eyes lying?"

"This can't be," another one of Detective Keith's men said, placing his hands on either side of his head. He took another close look at the pictures. "Nah, this fuckin' can't be!" he croaked, his words getting caught in his throat. "Something got to be wrong," he whispered. Then he turned toward the guilty one, who had his head hung low now.

I could see the hurt in all of the guys' faces. Street dudes or not, betrayal had the same effect on everyone. They all seemed suspended in time, like someone had just told them their mothers were dying or something. I could tell from the looks of sheer dismay on all of their faces, there could be nothing good in those photos.

My body went cold like someone had pumped ice water into my veins just watching the exchange. I could actually imagine the deep cut from that type of betrayal. I'd been betrayed before; I knew the hurt.

"The truth is all there," the Hispanic man insisted. "My boss expects you or your boss to handle this. We can't continue our business if you don't. Having a man inside that would set you up tells us your team is not airtight. We can't do business with anyone whose team is not airtight."

From what I had learned already from Kyle, I could surmise that the Hispanic man would be reporting back to his boss exactly how Detective Keith handled the situation. I knew in that moment his reputation and his boss's business dealings in the future depended on every single move he made now. Either he'd become known as a weak man in the business or a powerful force that wasn't having it. I guessed his traitorous worker had made the decision for him. It was a no-brainer.

My nerves were raggedy watching all of this shit go down. It wasn't even me in there and I actually felt vomit creeping up my esophagus. Fire burned in my chest and huge sweat beads raced down my back. I saw Kyle wipe sweat from his head too; he was feeling it as well. It was a whole lot to take in at once.

With his lips pursed and nostrils flaring, Detective Keith slipped his hand into his waistband. He wrapped his hand around the cold steel of a big black pistol and pulled it out slowly. I wondered if it was his service weapon and then immediately dismissed that thought of him being that stupid. My adrenaline rushed so fast as I watched Detective Keith turn and stalk toward his own men.

"Wait!" the guilty dude said, putting his hands up in front of him and attempting to halt Detective Keith's fury. He was too late.

The dirty detective walked right past his crew and up to the one member who'd been outed. None of them saw what was coming next. Without talking or screaming or warning, Detective Keith raised his weapon and placed it at the traitor's temple. Suddenly the room erupted and everyone started speaking at once. There was another angry hornet's nest of buzzing in the room. The gun wavered in the detective's hand as it kissed the skin of the traitor's forehead. More chaos erupted and different members of the crew were pulling out their weapons. Some pointed them at the detective and some at each other.

"What the fuck you doing, Redds?!" another one of his men barked.

Another one of their men followed Detective Keith's lead and trained his gun on the traitor too. But the other dude leveled his gun at Detective Keith's chest. My heart almost stopped. I knew shit was about to get real. If he shot, all kinds of shit was going to go down in the city— and I'd have it all on video. I silently cheered for myself.

"What the fuck!" the traitor growled, his hands up in surrender, weapon dangling off of his pointer finger. Clearly, he had no wins.

"Drop your weapon," Detective Keith said in a low, embittered whisper. "Drop your fucking weapon now!" Detective Keith screamed this time, his voice seemingly shaking the weak wooden shack walls.

I thought about my father for a hot minute. The way he died. The tragedy of it all. I didn't know if I wanted to witness that again, but I couldn't peel myself away.

"Do what he said, man," another dude told the traitor. He was outgunned. He knew if he made one false move, that would be his end.

"Explain yourself, motherfucker!" Detective Keith barked angrily, picking up the pictures and making them rain down around the traitor. If what was shown in the first set he'd dropped wasn't clear, this set must've made it unequivocally clear what had gone down.

"What the fuck?" Detective Keith barked again; his words seemed to catch in the back of his throat like he was hurt. It was the first sign of an emotion other than anger I'd seen the whole time.

"Is that you? You with dudes who are down with our worst enemy—motherfuckers who tried to put us out of business, who tried to kill us?" Detective Keith asked, his voice cracking some more like he was about to cry.

Everyone turned their guns to the traitor now. Even the Hispanic man and his crew did.

"Listen . . . I . . . I c-can explain," the traitor stammered now, his knees knocking together.

I knew from Kyle that in their line of business there really wasn't much more the traitor could say that could help his case. The pictures did not lie.

"Everybody in here was in agreement with me at one time or another. None of us wanted a dirty cop to be our boss. Don't front now! Come on now, y'all niggas remember what you said about how this nigga was a cop first and would always be a cop. So why is it that all y'all thought shit with him was suspect. A real street nigga would've never joined no police force . . . remember all that? You said that! Flip, remember you saying that this nigga Redds took over too fast and never gave us a chance to rise up. You even hinted at a setup on his part, saying he was police and you didn't trust this nigga! I'm not fucking crazy! What the fuck, man? Y'all not going to admit to shit now? I wasn't the only one that wanted to get rid of him. I did this for all of us! The other crew was going to take care of him and we were going to be on our own and make our own shit. I wasn't the only one. This was for the fam!" the traitor cried out, snitching on his crew while his voice rose and fell like a crying girl's.

Detective Keith reacted like he was taking a punch to the face every time the traitor said another thing out of his mouth.

I couldn't believe what I was watching. I looked away a few times but I did it in a way so that my feelings distract me.

"All y'all niggas stupid. I was put in the position by the boss of all bosses. If y'all don't like it, that's too fucking bad, because I am here to stay and you will all respect my authority," Detective Keith growled, flames flashing in his eyes. He ground the end of his gun on the traitor's temple.

"Please don't kill me," the traitor begged, trembling.

"I . . . I . . . can still help you. That man they got tied up is Arsenio's son. If you let them kill him, you will be a dead man walking." The traitor knew he only had minutes to live, so he was grasping at straws trying to save himself. The warning was the least he could do to make up for his cowardly betrayal.

"Shut the fuck up! Don't give me no fucking advice now, you fucking Judas!" Detective Keith growled, grinding his gun into the traitor's head even harder. The traitor closed his eyes . . . waiting for his ultimate fate.

I saw the other dudes, one by one, turn away. They all seemed devastated by their guy's betrayal, but even more about what they all knew would happen next. Kyle lowered his head as well. I had forgotten he basically knew all of those guys from the streets.

"Let this be an example to the next man who tries me," Detective Keith gritted, putting pressure on the trigger. "Go to hell, fucking traitor."

One powerful blast to the dome spun the traitor around in a slow pirouette as a spray of his blood and gray brain matter splashed onto the floor.

With the gun blast, I fell down onto the ground behind the house, wheezing for breath. I was paralyzed with fear. The same fear I felt when my father got shot in front of me. I felt like I was suffocating. Kyle crawled over to me and shook me.

"Get up. Let's go," he whispered harshly. "We got to get out of here before they see us. You can't fall apart now." He pulled me up onto my knees. I gripped my stomach and doubled over. Vomit spewed from my lips, just missing Kyle's shirt. My chest heaved like a beast in the wild after a fresh kill. I had just witnessed a cold-blooded murder by a cop. Something inside me seemed to snap apart. I knew all too well how violence could change lives. In that moment something awakened inside me. This wasn't going to be just about a story for Christian. This was going to be about changing things and bringing down violent criminals— like the ones that had changed my life in ways that I didn't realize until right then, because I had worked so many years to suppress it all.

4

THE AFTERMATH

I didn't sleep for days after I had witnessed that murder. Just like I thought would happen, I couldn't eat, sleep, think, interact with my family—nothing. Every time I tried to do anything, when I closed my eyes or even when they were open, I would see that guy's brains bust from his skull and his bloodied dead body hit that ground.

I knew I had to eventually return to work, but I wasn't looking forward to it. *The call-out excuses that I'm sick with the stomach virus* will run out sooner than later. With everything wearing heavily on my mind, I wasn't up for Christian and her shit at all. I was spooked, and everywhere I went in the days after the murder, I was looking over my shoulder, thinking people knew I was there. I worried that someone could tell I had the entire murder recorded. I was officially an eyewitness to a murder. Now, how crazy is that?

Kyle and I had gotten out of there before the dirty detective and his people left and could see us. From the moment we'd gotten back to the car, wheezing and huffing and puffing for air, I could not stop wondering what they'd do with the guy's body. The thought of them leaving someone there to rot and decompose to the point that he couldn't even have a decent funeral had nagged at me. It didn't matter to me if the guy had been a traitor to his people—or that I knew he was a drug-dealing criminal—he was still a human being. Our ride back to my mother's house that day had been eerily silent. I don't think Kyle or I anticipated the mental space we'd be transported to after witnessing that cold-blooded killing.

I'd stayed in my old room for two days, only coming out for a few hours. Kyle had come by and told me that everyone in the street was talking about how the dude that had been murdered in the shack had gone missing. It had been on the news and everything, but only we and the killers knew the real deal. I could barely look my mother in the eye. She knew we were going to be out there covering dangerous territory, but I'm sure she didn't expect that we'd be witnesses to a murder. I could tell she was suspicious that we were hiding something from her, but she was trying hard not to ask. My mother had been buzzing around and trying to make small talk. That was her way. I think the guilt of her past kept her from prying all the way.

Kyle knocked on the spare bedroom door, where I'd been holed up for the past couple days.

"Come in," I called to him, pulling the covers up over me.

"What up, twin?" Kyle asked, bopping in the room. I could smell the weed emanating from him before he even sat down on the end of the bed. I knew how he'd been coping with seeing what we saw.

"I'm just here. Not really sleeping, and dreading going back to work," I groaned. "What about you?"

"I'm maintaining. People in the streets are talking. They're asking around about when the last time anyone seen dude. Ole girl, his baby moms came up to our spot asking me directly if I knew of any spots he might've been going to, or anywhere out of town he might've gone," Kyle said, shaking his head. "Shit is sad, man. I hate to see his son with no pops like that. I grew up the same way . . . I know that pain," he continued.

I sat up and looked at Kyle seriously. "Damn, even his baby mother is out scouring the streets. Where the fuck are the cops?" I replied. "That's how they do us?"

"You know what it is with the Norfolk PD. They did a few knock-and-talks, but they ain't going too far. One, this is a black dude we talking about, and they don't give a hot damn about our lives. Two, you know who got people up in that missing person squad and have already probably heard this shit and had the clean cops close their case right out," Kyle said. He sighed and shook his head. "This nigga ain't even going to get a proper burial because we the only ones who even know where his body is at and we ain't telling shit," Kyle said, giving me the eye. "You hear me? We are not telling anyone shit about seeing what happened and where that body is at. You got it?"

I shook my head slightly but didn't say another word. My mind was racing a million miles a minute. I was thinking, maybe if I called in an anonymous tip to the police, they could go in and locate the body. And then I could report on it as a placeholder until I broke the news on the bigger case, revealing the double life of the potential future mayor. It could possibly all work out in the end. The dude would get a burial, his baby mother and kids would get some closure, and I would get the first of many good stories to come. I was thinking hard on it, but I wouldn't dare tell Kyle. At least not yet.

"It's crazy, man. These street cats out here asking if any-body know who would've wanted to hurt him or rob him for any reason. Personally, I was annoyed as shit about all of the questions. Why would they assume any of us knew the answers? What would make people believe that we would tell them shit anyway?" Kyle complained some more, pulling out his trusty pick and picking his hair, which was his new nervous tick.

Right away I wondered if Detective Keith had already somehow disposed of the body, and even my anonymous tip would be for nothing then. Just the thought of that dirty cop getting away with murder, scot-free, made me shudder and feel sick to my stomach. As crazy as the thought was, I felt like I needed to do something more . . . get in deeper. The urgency I was feeling to bring this crime ring down was keeping me up at night and haunting me all during the day.

After Kyle talked some more, he finally left. Thank God. I loved my brother to the end of earth, but some-times I didn't want to know everything about the streets. I might've been better off not knowing that the dude who'd been killed had a family, just like my father did when he was murdered. It was tough to think about. And even tougher to feel like I couldn't really do anything about it.

I waited until I thought my mother was asleep to go into the kitchen to have some chamomile tea. I was hoping something warm in my stomach and the soothing proper-ties in chamomile would help me finally get some sleep—especially because I was going to have to return to the office tomorrow. I was standing before the refrigerator with my back turned, getting the milk for my tea.

"Baby girl?" my mother said, and touched my shoulder from behind me. I almost jumped out of my skin as if a bolt of lightning had struck me. My mother snatched her hand away quickly and took a few steps backward.

"Did I scare you?" she asked, her eyes wide and her hand on her chest.

I swallowed hard and put on a fake smile, and I put the milk down out of my shaking hands.

"Um . . . no. I was just getting some tea and didn't hear you coming, so I was a little thrown off when you touched me. I've just been feeling a little stressed with everything going on . . . you know, with work and the pressure still," I said, my voice shaky. She'd scared the hell out of me—if I was being honest. My nerves were on a hairpin trigger. I couldn't stop my hands from shaking. I shoved them in the pockets of my bathrobe and even that didn't help. I couldn't let my mother see too much, because she sometimes took her concern for Kyle and me to another level.

"I know you have been stressed. I also know you were talking about letting your brother help you get a story," my mother said, one part sympathetic, the other part suspicious. I looked at her strangely as if to say, *What is the question under your statement?* I guess my mother sensed it or either read my mind and the expression on my face.

"What I'm saying is that there is something going on. I can tell from you and from Kyle, both walking around here and looking like you saw a ghost each. I can hear you at night and him too. Neither one of you are sleeping very soundly these past few nights. Remember, I gave birth to y'all, and when something is going on, I can feel it. So, if there is something, I need to know, you better tell me. I don't want any surprises and the only way I can help either of you is if I know everything . . . nothing being held back," my mother continued. A pang of guilt flitted through my chest and belly. I wanted to tell her so badly what we'd seen, and how it had been awful to watch someone die in the same way my father had died, but telling my mother about the murder wasn't an option. I couldn't take the risk of what she might do or how she might react to the information. If that ever got out in the streets, Kyle and I would be running for our lives, for sure.

"Nope. There's nothing going on, except what I've already said," I answered, shaking my head emphatically. "Just that good ole work stress getting to me, that's all." I had to sip the hot-ass tea to keep from spilling the beans. Obviously, I was itching to talk to someone. These were the moments I wished I would've continued therapy after we left the foster care system. Back then, they forced us to get counseling, so I had always been against it.

"Yeah, okay. I know better, but I'll wait until you're ready," my mother came back, her mouth twisted to the side.

"Right, cuz you're such a mom," I said sarcastically.

"Don't go getting snippy and nasty about it, just because I am concerned. I know I wasn't always the best mother, but I am *still* your mother, and my love and concern for you and Kyle never wavered . . . ever," my mother shot back. I could hear crackles of hurt stringing through her words.

I lowered my eyes and stared down into my cup of tea. Admittedly, my smart remark was a low blow and meant to jab at my mother. I *was* sorry, but I couldn't bring myself to say "I'm sorry" to her. Sometimes my leftover anger for her for the past crept out at times like this. I knew she was right. She had always acknowledged the wrong she'd done, but it wasn't easy for Kyle and me to just accept sometimes. We had suffered a lot of hurt and pain while she tried to fight her addiction. I'd learned over the years that addiction is a disease and needed constant treatment, but I wasn't always just accepting of it. Like now, she wanted to be all concerned, when she wasn't the years we lived in foster care and got abused.

"So, like I said, I already know something is up and I'm here when you're ready to tell me what it is," my mother continued. I must say, she didn't give up easily when she felt strongly about something. I guess that was where Kyle and I got it from.

"You're right. I know you care. But this time, you're going to have to ignore whatever you think you know and go with it," I said, annoyed that she kept insisting that she knew something was wrong.

"I won't ignore, I'll just wait," my mother replied, her eyebrows in high arches on her face.

"Oh, my God, you just don't quit," I grunted, still on the defensive. It was bad enough how I was feeling—nauseous, not sleeping, worried all of the time. I was coming apart at the seams and it was clear. I had to get away from my mother before I gave in and just blurted out the details of the murder. This was definitely more than I had bargained for, just to get a good story. And where was Christian? Somewhere sitting on a high horse, waiting for me to come in and crown her the head bitch of ratings. The thought infuriated me all over again.

"Well, like I said, I am your mother and part of that is never giving up when you know your kids are in distress. Now, to change the subject, I made your favorite . . . German chocolate cake. Have some and enjoy it. Maybe it'll be so good, you'll finally want to share with me what is going on," my mother said, repeating the same thing again, as if something about my decision was going to change. She was still eyeing me suspiciously. *She's a damn trip!*

"Thanks for the cake, Mama," I said, sounding as calm as I could. I knew she was dead serious about not giving up. I was going to have to break down and go home and be alone. If I stayed at my mother's house, she was going to wear me down with questions. Shit, at this point I didn't know if I'd ever come back. That was, of course, until the next scary thing happened while I chased this story.

5

MAKING THE RIGHT CHOICES

It took me another day before I actually went back to my apartment. And it was another two after that before I was ready to return to the office to see what the atmosphere was like. I wasn't ready to tell Christian about my story prospect just yet. Or so I thought.

As soon as I rounded the corner near the main floor of the news station studio, I could hear her voice rising and falling on waves of anger and vituperative words. Her usual. I froze, hid at the side of the wall, peeked around the corner, and listened for a moment. For a change I wasn't the one standing there while Christian yelled, screamed, threatened, and told me how terrible I was. It felt kind of good to be watching and not receiving this time around.

"Are you a fucking idiot or what?" Christian snapped from the executive producer's chair she occupied at WXOT-TV. She was so drunk with power it dripped off of her every word. Her face looked like a witch's right before the witch threw you into her burning cauldron of hot liquid. Oh, my goodness, Christian was even uglier when she was mad like this.

"I mean, I can't send you to do one fucking thing without a bunch of instructions. How do you ever expect to rise to actual reporting if you can't even put decent segments together?" Christian continued her tirade. "I guess they're always pushing you people up the ladder and out front like some affirmative-action bullshit, but if they knew half of what I know—which is that you have half a damn brain—they'd keep your ass right where I have you. Where's Khloé or my favorite, Amber? People who studied hard and don't mind getting out there and getting their hands dirty for a story," Christian went on, destroying someone with her words. This was what she lived for daily.

A flash of heat came over me at the mention of my name. I guess it wasn't a bad thing that Christian had said my name in sort of a complimentary way. Being mentioned in the same sentence with Amber made me cringe, though.

Liza, the entertainment-desk production assistant, who had the unfortunate luck to be the current victim of Christian's tyrannical rant, looked like she was going to cry. Her caramel-colored face and neck turned deep red with embarrassment under the scrutinizing stares of the crew. She let out a long sigh that blew a few scraggly pieces of her naturally curly hair out of her face. The entire back of her blouse was soaked with sweat and she looked queasy, like she'd vomit any minute. I knew that feeling. Watching her made the hairs on the back of my neck stand up.

"I'm sorry, Ms. Aniston," Liza said weakly as she scrambled around, nervously gathering all of her papers into her arms. A few pieces floated to the floor at her feet. "I . . . I . . . thought this was what you wanted. You said anything about the Kardashians or the Carters that hadn't already been reported on b-by *TMZ* or *Access Hollywood,* so . . . I . . . I . . . th-thought . . ." Liza was stuttering, going in literal circles.

"And you think a story about them hating each other or about their children competing in the media hasn't been done before?" Christian scoffed. "That's your problem, girl. You *think* you know too much about what I want, instead of getting out there and actually getting me what I want. You've been here awhile now, this is unacceptable. I can only conclude one thing . . . that you're stupid," Christian said.

Liza looked like she'd died inside a thousand times. It was hard to watch. With every insult Christian hurled, I cringed and winced. If I could feel the pain of it, imagine what Liza was feeling.

"Get her away from me, please." Christian waved her hand dismissively. "I have no time for half-wits and dimwits, which I seemed to be surrounded by these days."

I exhaled and shivered as I remembered the feeling of taking that same type of verbal abuse, over and over again. It was the kind of browbeating that could make a bitch off herself at home. Liza finally scurried away like a child who'd just been released from time-out in the corner. It was a shame that we had to come to work and endure that type of abuse.

Christian put her handheld mirror in front of her face to check her hair and makeup. After a tirade like that, I guess she had to make sure her face hadn't fallen off. Christian's wrinkled white skin needed more work to look like something than anyone I'd ever seen. The makeup artist at the studio worked hard to put a good face on Christian daily. Although she was only forty-two, Christian looked more like sixty-two. I often found myself thinking, *If she were black, she wouldn't crack.* At least not like that. Sometimes I wondered if her evil ways were what made her look so old, so fast, too. I shrugged. Who cares? She was a tyrant, and that was the conclusion everyone at the studio had come to all on our own. There wasn't one person at

WXOT-TV that hadn't been victim to Christian Aniston. Oh, maybe except . . . Amber Darby, my archenemy in life.

Just as Christian put her mirror down, I watched as Amber sauntered over with a smug smile on her face. Her pale white skin gleamed with perfectly applied makeup, and her hair lay limp in the flat way those white girls I refer to as "Beckys" did. Just hanging there, blah and stringy, so that they were always using their hands to move it out of there face or push it behind their ears. Amber thought she was the shit at the station.

I hated Amber, and it was that simple. I followed her with my eyes, with steam coming out of my ears. The close-fitting, bright orange wrap dress Amber wore played up her striking blue eyes. She had graduated from Christian's personal assistant to an actual on-screen reporting entertainment journalist. She replaced a black woman named Sandra. I watched from the sidelines with my insides boiling, as if someone had just lit a fire in my chest. It wasn't jealousy either. It was a real, deep hatred.

"More mistakes?" Amber asked Christian, following Liza with her eyes as the girl scrambled for the door. "Damn, what a difference a year makes. She went from doing no wrong to doing everything wrong. I guess she has been exposed for the dummy that she was all along," Amber sniped, boldly climbing into the chair next to Christian's. I shook my head and curled my hands into fists. If only I could run out there and punch that bitch in the face, I would have.

"Ugh, please. That little girl gets on my last nerve. I mean, I can't see how any of these little dummies keep a job. None of them are capable. I might have to get back on-screen to save this station if none of them will step it up," Christian replied, trying to stay still while the masseuse, whom she'd had the station hire just for her, kneaded her shoulder muscles. Watching her in action was really something to behold. I shook my head some more. I was surrounded by a bunch of dingy bitches at work. They were airhead hos, with MBAs in communication and journalism, with fake-ass tits, and with a desire to become the next big thing. But their ship had sailed, because I will be the next "It girl" around here. I can promise them that.

"Well, that's why you're the queen on the throne now, and the former executive producer is working in some public-access station's back room. She hired all of these half-a-brain people and now you have to clean up her mess," Amber snickered. "Maybe she should have taken them all with her—Liza . . . that other girl . . . what's her name . . . um . . . Khloé. They don't deserve the spotlight, if you ask me," Amber went on, looking at her nails in the pretentious, snobby way she always did.

I jumped at the sound of my name, and her saying it made me bite down harder on my lip, which I'd been already gnawing. I bit down so hard that I drew blood and could taste it.

Amber knew my name damn well, because she hated me, and I hated her. She was so jealous of me that she'd do anything to get rid of me or to make me look bad in Christian's eyes. Amber knew I was smarter, prettier, and more popular than she was with everyone else at the station, except for Christian.

Christian and Amber shared a laugh at the idea of our old executive producer shuffling around in some dusty, off-brand television studio, looking for a story to report on, with Liza and me going around in circles with her. Amber would've loved nothing more than to have that happen. *Over my dead body* was what I always told myself. Amber was not going to win by getting rid of me. I wasn't having it. I've built so much since I've been here. Made a lot of sacrifices too.

"Thank God for you and me, because we have the sense we were born with . . . These others must've missed that line." Christian had followed up with a joke of her own, but that shit wasn't funny to me.

In fact, my heart lurched in my chest; it started throbbing so hard, it hurt. However, I stood my ground a little bit longer. I wanted to hear how far these two would go with their insults. I wanted them to give me a reason. Give me more ammunition.

"They missed that line!" Amber echoed, raising her hand to slap five with Christian. More raucous laughter ensued between the mentor and her protégée. Amber wanted to be just like Christian. I'd watched Amber take copious notes each day on Christian's wardrobe and then she would go out and purchase either the same items or things that were strikingly similar. She even tried to do her hair like Christian's. When the boss got a new look, which was pretty old-ladyish for a young girl like Amber, she would still come in looking like a Christian clone. In fact, one of the station hands had told me he'd heard Amber quietly repeating those words to herself each morning, like a mantra: "Think it and you will be it. I'm going to be just like you. Just like you, Christian Aniston. I'm going to be so much like you, they won't need you."

I could tell that Christian loved the fact that she was able to take her old boss Lucy Cole's job as executive producer of the station. Christian also relished the fact that she was able to change the tide at the station, where uplifting and hiring minorities had been Lucy's priority after years of discrimination against us. Christian would have nothing of the sort. She had quickly changed the faces of the people in the important roles to ones that looked like hers—pale, pale, pale. Because of Christian's tactics, Lucy's role was missed instantly. But there was no turning back.

Christian's newfound clout and power at WXOT-TV was rumored to be because she'd slept her way to the top and brought in exclusive stories, which I heard she had embellished all along the way. They couldn't risk letting Christian run to a rival station, so they not only gave Christian her boss's job, they also let Christian hire and fire whomever she wanted. She was running things . . . literally. I knew that wasn't going to change anytime soon, so either I was going to get on board and fight for the prime-time spot, or I was going to be fired or worse, have to quit out of sheer embarrassment.

I finally stepped from behind the wall as if I hadn't been standing there listening to these two racist bitches carry on from the start. I was glad to break up their little mean-girl gossip party. Although I wished I could break it up by breaking Amber's face. *Whew!* My disdain for that girl ran deep.

"Ah, would you look at what the cat dragged in," Christian said, turning her attention and vile attitude toward me. She did the sarcastic Nancy Pelosi extended-arms, finger-tap, clapping motion. Oh, my God! I wanted to curse her out so badly.

Instead, I swallowed hard and rolled my eyes a little. Just a little, not enough to show a lot of attitude, but just enough to say I was not in the mood for the shenanigans. It was too early in the fucking morning for it.

"Morning, Christian," I grumbled. I still wasn't sleeping, so I was cranky and certainly was not in the mood for the bullshit. "Just letting you know I'm back."

"And just where have you been?" Amber asked sarcastically.

"I took some sick days but I was also given time away from the office to work on my story," I shot back, instinctively rolling my neck like a homegirl would. If eyes could kill, Amber would've exploded on the spot, like I had put a grenade up her ass, which, of course, would've made my day run so much smoother.

"Hmph," Amber mumbled, and folded her arms across her chest. "Missing from work, looking a mess, can't find a good story . . . need I go on?"

"Listen, you don't want none today, Amber. Oh, trust me," I said, pounding my left fist into my right palm. "You don't want no smoke over here, girl."

"Enough, ladies," Christian interjected, turning her eyes back to me. "So, Miss Khloé, what do you have for me today?" Christian asked, rubbing her hands together like a greedy kid in a candy store. My eyes darted straight over to Amber and I gave her a look as if to say, *Get the hell out of here, you snake.* I wasn't about to reveal anything about my news story in front of that backstabbing bitch Amber. She'd backstabbed me once before, and whenever I was forced to be around Amber, my mind automatically shot backward to that day . . .

It had been a hot-ass, heat wave–type July day in the Norfolk area and I was flustered after I had come outside to find that my piece-of-shit car had overheated for the fifth time in two weeks. I was brand-new at the station, and there I stood, in front of the open hood, while steam literally shot up from under the car hood like a hot-springs geyser. My cheeks felt sunburned and sweat had plastered my hair to my head like I had styled it that way with gel. The sun was beaming down on me unmercifully; my body was drenched in so much sweat, you would've thought I'd just run through a sprinkler. Water poured off of me—

from my armpits, down my legs, between my breasts, and down my back. I got hotter and hotter with each movement I made, and, of course, these thick thighs of mine were rubbing together. I had just broken up with Dominic, my boyfriend, so I couldn't call him to come and help me with the car. I had called Kyle's cell phone over ten times with no answer or callback, which was odd and certainly not like him.

"Where the hell is Kyle when I need his ass," I huffed. I called him six or seven more times before I got so angry, I felt like throwing my phone on the ground and smashing it. But had I done that, then I'd be broke with no car *and* no phone. You would think Kyle might realize I was calling him for an emergency and answer his damn phone. But still, nothing. My mother didn't believe in cell phones and I knew she was at her NA meeting during that time anyway, so there was no use in me calling her old-school house phone. No luck. I was out of luck.

I had finally flopped down on a tiny piece of curb next to my car to try and figure out my next moves. I hadn't gotten my first paycheck from the station yet, which meant I was still struggling financially with ten dollars in my pocketbook and broke as a joke. I certainly did not have enough money to call any kind of mechanic company to come help me with the car. I sat there with my head in my hands for almost ten minutes before a pair of feet stopped in front of me.

At first, I didn't look up. I looked down at the little shiny, patent leather work flats from Target. I knew where they came from, because I had several pairs myself. I crinkled my face in confusion and sucked my teeth. I wasn't in the mood for anybody and their small-talk conversation. Then I decided to look up and see who it was, so I could dismiss them really quick. It was Amber. I kind of felt uncomfortable with her looking down at me like I was a charity case, so I jumped to my feet.

"What's going on, Khloé? You look like you're having a time-out here," she said, a little too cheery for my liking.

"My car is acting up," I answered, mumbling the obvious. Amber could clearly see what was going on, so I was confused about why she would ask. We were both new to the station and trying to figure things out with working and life in general. I didn't know much about her, but she seemed nice enough. I mean, she had stopped to find out what was going on, when several others of my coworkers had just either waved and kept it moving or avoided looking in my direction, like they didn't see me in need of help.

Amber had pulled out her car keys. "Well, I can give you a ride home or to a shop if you need me to," she had offered kindly. "No use in you standing out here frying in the sun. C'mon," she continued.

"Oh, my goodness, would you really? That's so kind of you, Amber. I'll buy you lunch for a few days to repay you," I had said, perking up and happily taking her up on her offer. She was right: Standing out there wasn't going to solve a thing, and I'd already fried in the sun long enough. It felt like I had almost run to Amber's car—that was how desperate I was to get the hell out of that scorching heat. Amber had a nice little C-Class Mercedes-Benz with tan leather interior. It was a comfortable little ride. I had quickly assessed that she was the spoiled white princess type who'd probably gotten her car as a birthday gift when she turned sixteen. Still, I had been super grateful for her offer to take me home so I could find Kyle to hustle up a way to fix my piece-of-crap car.

"Thank God," I had huffed out as the cool air from Amber's air conditioner hit my face and body. I rested my head back on the headrest, let the air blow in my face, and took several deep breaths. Amber turned down her rock music, which had immediately started blasting when she started the ignition.

"Sorry about that," she said awkwardly, as if she knew that a black girl like me would not like that noise that she called music. But I could care less about her music choice. That was the furthest thing from my mind. So we sat in uncomfortable silence for a few long seconds.

"So, what are you working on?" Amber had asked, being the first to break the quiet in the car.

I opened my eyes and sat up a bit with excitement because I had a chance to speak to someone about my work, since Kyle and my mother were never really that interested in hearing it.

"Oh, my gosh, I found a story lead about a suspected kidnapping that might've just happened. This girl Lisa is the daughter of a criminal court judge and no one has seen her . . . She's missing. Her father, the judge, is thought to have lots of enemies and they're starting to worry that this is not a missing person's case, but may be a kidnapping. I'm still working up the information, but it is a solid lead. I should be bringing it to Christian by the end of this week," I had blabbed. I was honestly and innocently elated to share my story lead with Amber. It was refreshing to have someone to talk shop with outside work. My guard had been completely down around her, which wasn't at all like the normal, guarded me.

"Really?" Amber had asked, sounding interested. "Tell me more," she insisted. She was becoming giddy by the second. "Where are they from? What court is the father a judge out of? Which police are working on it?" She asked a million questions, and I happily and freely answered them all.

I had gone on and on about the story idea and how I

was going to be loved at the station for it. I told her that I had already pulled some police documents and done some background research on the father. I'd told Amber my plan on winning Christian over and how my ultimate goal was to nab that six o'clock spot on live TV. Amber had listened intently and gave me several words of encouragement. She'd seemed genuinely happy for me and even offered to help me with anything I needed . . . including rides in the field or rides home after work. In the days after she'd given me the ride home, she would come around me at the station and ask more and more questions about my story idea. In the moment I hadn't thought anything of it. She seemed like she could be a friend to me. A trusting coworker. I guess I had been naïve enough to think that Amber would have the same type of morals and loyalty that I had. Turned out, I was in the business of "kill or be killed." No one went by a set of rules. Everyone was for themselves, and the sooner I realized that, the better off I would be.

6

CUTTHROAT GAMES

Four days after Amber had saved my life in the station parking lot, I'd rushed into the news station with my notes for my story, ready to present to Christian. I was sure the story was solid, and that Christian was going to be elated about it. When I'd finally made it down the long hallway to the main station floor, where all of us new assistants usually gathered to let Christian hear out next story idea, I saw a small crowd gathered there already. They all seemed to be watching something intently. I wanted to know what was going on, so I pushed my way through to see. I wedged between two other new, young reporters to see what the buzz was all about. As soon as I heard it, I felt faint. It was as if a hundred bombs had exploded in my ears. I quickly found out that it was Amber's voice that had everyone, including Christian, enthralled:

"In breaking news Norfolk police are reporting that they are searching tonight for a missing teenager, Lisa Benton, the eighteen-year-old daughter of criminal court judge Marc Benton. It has been over two weeks since anyone has

seen Lisa, who, at first, was suspected of being a runaway.
Benton and his wife insist that their daughter would never
run away from home. The prominent judge told us that he
last spoke to his daughter on her cell phone the night before she went missing. Judge Benton told Norfolk detectives that he and his wife have a great relationship with
their daughter, and it is not like Lisa to leave for this long
without contacting them.

"Police have spoken to a limited number of witnesses so
far who say the young woman was last seen at an unnamed
posh restaurant, where her parents say she went to celebrate her upcoming high school graduation with friends.
Police have not revealed whether or not they have spoken
to any of the missing girl's friends who attended the dinner
as well. The teen's late-model Audi SUV has not been located at this time. Judge Benton and the Norfolk police are
asking that anyone with information about Lisa Benton's
possible whereabouts contact the tip line at 877-MISS-
ING."

That was my story! Those were my words! I had pre-
viewed my newscast to Amber exactly like she was saying
it to the group, including Christian. I had immediately
began shaking all over. Heat rose from my feet and burst
through the top of my head. My mind was telling me to
bust through the crowd and snatch that bitch by her hair
and fuck her up. But, for some reason, my body was not following the directions of the thoughts racing through my
brain. Instead, I just stood there, suspended in time, choking
on every stolen word Amber uttered out of her thieving-ass
mouth.

A tornado of emotions swirled inside me. I had felt unsteady on my feet. Suddenly I could no longer hear Amber
practicing my story for broadcast later that evening; all I
could hear were alarm bells ringing in my head. My heart

rate sped up so fast, it made my head hurt. I felt like I was going to actually faint. My first instinct was to make a nasty scene, because it was warranted. But that would've put me at risk of losing my job and my reputation in the business. I played the scenario out in my mind, over and over: *Crazy black girl beats up white girl and accuses her of stealing a story.* I'd be dubbed the "angry black girl" and never land another news job in my life. I'd certainly never get on the 6:00 p.m. news desk, which had been my goal the whole time.

In that moment my entire body was trembling, and then I realized I was standing there amongst my other peers on the verge of tears and looking crazy. *I've been through worse,* I told myself. I was stronger than that, because I came from the rough. I remember as a child going hungry. Gotten my ass beat up by chicks in my old neighborhood when I was a kid. A few of my boyfriends cheated on me. So this shit, right here, can't be nothing more than a minor setback. I told myself to pull it together.

Here I was thinking Amber and I had started building a friendship, and all along she was stabbing me in the front and back. I'd even grabbed lunch for us both, just like I said I would, the day she gave me the ride. I always kept my promises. I was always loyal and trusting to a certain extent too. I had been planning to surprise Amber with what she'd told me was her favorite meal—shrimp and pasta from the Cheesecake Factory. Instead, she'd surprised me with a betrayal so huge. Tears had involuntarily begun to roll down my face before I could help it. I quickly and angrily swiped at the tears, pissed at myself for being weak in that moment. I whirled on the balls of my feet and pushed my way back through the crowd, which had been watching Amber in awe.

"Hey, Khloé . . . what's wrong with you?" Joe, one of

the station's backstage hands, came after me and asked. Suddenly my body itched with the heat of shame and embarrassment. *You damn crybaby! Now someone has seen you crying like a silly child!* I had silently chastised myself.

I quickly swiped my hands over my face and turned around to face him. With my chest heaving up and down, and my entire body trembling like a leaf in a wild storm, I finally willed myself to be calm.

"Allergies kicking my ass," I lied, sniffling and wiping my face again with my hands.

"I understand," Joe said, with some doubt curling on his lips. "Well, feel better," he said, following up, but still looking at me strangely.

I had almost run away from him. I wanted to get out of there so badly. I got to the staff lounge, where our refrigerator and table were located. I walked over and grabbed the bag containing my lunch and Amber's. I raced into our common area, where we all had small lockers. I took Amber's food, opened her locker, and dumped the sauce-covered pasta and shrimp all over her belongings. Even that hadn't made me feel any better. I felt lost. I spun around a few times like a madwoman before I'd finally gotten my bearings. I located my knapsack, grabbed it and my cell phone, and rushed to the station's exit. I didn't know where I was going, but I knew I had to get out of there before I caught a case.

Dumb! Dumb! Dumb! I had chanted in my head. *I can't believe it. How could I be that stupid to trust Amber or anyone with my story?*

Who, but me, would trust someone they barely knew, just because she offered them a goddamn ride home? I beat myself up royally for that. No wonder all of the senior reporters at the station had been so standoffish and snobby toward all of us newbies; they didn't trust each other or us newbies.

I had raced to my car and got in. I started to drive aimlessly. I couldn't even think straight. The tears began to flow again. I couldn't believe this had happened to me. At first, I thought about calling Kyle and having him get some dudes from the neighborhood to set Amber up: They could rob that bitch and beat her ass a little bit. Break her arm, snatch a clump of hair from her scalp, give her dumb ass a busted lip and black eye. Spray-painting her car would've done the job too. I'm sure that probably would've made me feel better, but I decided against it, thinking it would've been too risky for Kyle.

Then I thought about marching right into Christian's office and telling her exactly what Amber had done. How she had stolen the very story I'd told her about. But the way Christian was, there was no telling whose side she would've taken. Then I thought about starting a rumor at the studio about that bitch Amber, telling everyone she had some incurable STD that she'd gotten during her days as a prostitute. That would've just made me look like I was jealous and petty. None of my ideas for revenge were going to pan out, because I was too emotional. Plotting someone's downfall never works out if you're emotional. I learned that a long time ago. So, what should I do?

After driving around for a while, I finally came up with a way to deal with how I was feeling about Amber and what she'd done. "You fucked the wrong person, Amber. You may have gotten away with this one, but I'll show you who will really win in the end," I growled out loud as if somehow Amber could hear me. At that moment I had decided that instead of being the stereotypical angry black girl, and giving Amber the satisfaction of playing the victim, like white girls loved to do, I would slowly and methodically plot my revenge against that bitch. I had decided that I would destroy Amber slowly and watch her career crumble to ashes, but not before I showed Christian who the real star reporter was. I had something to prove and I'm gonna make sure that Christian is sitting in the front row.

Now I stood there wrapped up in the memory and feeling all the same distrust for Amber. She stared at me just as hard as I stared at her. I wasn't backing down from my hatred of her, and, clearly, she wasn't either.

"I'm working on a few things," I answered Christian vaguely, looking at Amber through squinted eyes the whole time. I wanted that bitch to know she would never hear a story idea out of my mouth. Amber knew I hated her. She'd tried to act like she couldn't, for the life of her, understand why, but she knew what she'd done.

Christian finally picked up on it. She heard the rumors. She knew what Amber had done to me back then. Christian turned toward Amber and smiled. "Give us a minute, sweetie," she sang sweetly. I never heard Christian speak to anyone as nicely as she spoke to Amber all of the time.

"See you around," Amber said snidely, bumping my shoulder as she passed me. I bit down into my jaw to keep myself from swinging on that skinny bitch. I could've beat her ass mercilessly, and Christian would not have been able to pull me off that bitch either. What I would've unleashed on her would have been years of torture and pain I suffered growing up. She would've felt every blow I would've lunged at her. There was no question that I would've been escorted out of here in handcuffs. And in doing that, I would've let her win, and I couldn't allow that to happen. So I released a windstorm of breath and looked at Christian.

"Okay, so we are alone now. You looked like you wanted to tell me about something big," Christian followed up, suddenly all business again. She really was the Devil in a dress.

"Well, I do, sort of. This is one you wouldn't expect. It doesn't hit too far from home either," I said, boldly taking a seat next to my boss, just like Amber had done. Fuck it, if Amber could do it, I dared Christian to say something to me for doing it. I would file an Equal Employment Opportunity lawsuit so fast, her wrinkled neck would snap. This would not have looked good on the station. And especially on Christian, since she's the boss.

"Okay . . . let's hear it then," Christian prodded.

I had told myself I wasn't going to tell her too much, but I started to get caught up in the competition of the moment. I wasn't going to let Amber best me in Christian's eyes. I needed to prove that I was worthy of being there, even more than Amber.

"I have a strong lead on a certain mayoral candidate," I said, partially dropping the bomb. "I'll just say that the person has some real integrity issues that would make for very good reporting."

Christian perked up and sat up erect in her chair. "Continue," she said, tapping her big horse teeth with her nail, like she sometimes did when she was thinking.

"Well, like I said, right now it is just a strong lead. But my spies gave me some pretty reliable information that this certain candidate is up to a lot of shady dealings. I mean, this tea is so hot, it could burn down a house. The station phones will be ringing, and the ratings will be skyrocketing when we break this," I relayed, trying my best not to give too much away.

"Okay, but what is it? Who is it? I mean, I need more to make sure you're not spinning your wheels and would have wasted your time and mine in the end," Christian asked, moving to the edge of her chair and sticking out her neck toward me as if she could suck the information out of my brain. It wasn't going to work. I could just imagine her getting ahold of my story and mentioning it to Amber. I already learned my lesson. I won't be fooled again. Ever.

One thing about me, I was a quick study. After Lucy hired me, she'd taken me under her wing for a bit and I had blossomed. But when Christian came on board after me, I had fallen to the bottom of the popular pile, unless I could bring her something juicy. I recalled what Christian had said to me, over and over again: *"Sometimes you have to go out there and make your own exclusive. Seduce a few people. Stalk some people. Whatever it takes. Even stealing sometimes."*

As I had made my way up the ranks at the station, I had gone home each night, studied my craft, and practiced how to speak like a real on-air news anchor.

"You'll get all of the details soon. It'll be the juicy exclusive you're looking for," I assured her. "But I won't tell you anymore while we are here . . . in mixed company," I continued, looking over my shoulder for emphasis. I turned back to Christian with a telling smirk on my face. "You know these walls have ears, eyes, legs, and arms too. I learned from some of the best in the business—don't ever tell your executive producer too much. That way you'll always have your I-didn't-even-know defense when the shit hits the fan," I said to Christian, looking around the room suspiciously. "And trust me, with this one . . . the shit will definitely be hitting the fan."

"Well, okay, Miss Khloé. These are the things I like to hear," Christian said, smiling like the Cheshire cat. "Sounds like you have it covered, and I could only hope so. Everyone's job is on the line here."

I nodded my understanding. "Oh, but there is a little tidbit you'd want to know about something else I'm thinking about working on as well," I said, moving closer to Christian as if this one was a secret too. "I heard that our rival station's director is having an affair. I have proof that your nemesis is sleeping around," I whispered, darting my eyes around the room to make believe I was making sure no one else was privy to our conversation.

Christian raised her eyebrows, and her lips dropped open slightly. "Wait. What?" Christian said, and climbed down from the studio chair. "You know for sure?"

"No. I didn't see him, but my special little snoops said they spotted him coming out of another woman's house. And, even though he had on dark shades and a baseball cap, my special little spies confirmed that it was him," I lied.

"Well, I'll be damned!" Christian was flabbergasted by the news. She put her hands on her hips and gnawed on her bottom lip as she started pacing in front of the chairs a bit. "Are you going to work on this one too?"

"Yes, so please keep this between us," I said, knowing damn well she wasn't going to keep it between us at all. She had been telling Amber everything about everyone in the studio, even after she knew that Amber was a story thief. Christian was thinking, I could tell by how her eyes fluttered and she tapped her teeth. I was thinking too, because I wanted to see just how far she would backstab someone to propel her little protégée forward. This was going to be interesting to see play out. I was ready.

"Call your sources. I need to know more details. I have to break this story before any other station does," Christian urged.

"Already on it. I should know more soon. I'm working on all angles. I took what you said about great stories very seriously," I replied like a dutiful soldier. "I am going to make you proud, Christian," I said, laying my phony shit on thick for good measure.

Christian's eyes went wide. "Damn. You don't play. I

taught you so fucking well, it makes me almost orgasmic," Christian replied excitedly.

I put on a phony smile, but I was thinking in my head, *Bitch, you didn't teach me shit, and don't be saying I make you orgasmic. Yuck.* I didn't say what I was thinking.

"You sure did," I replied instead, lying some more. I wanted to tell that bitch the only thing she taught me was how to continue to play dirty in the reporting business in order to get where I want to be in my career.

"Darla!" Christian called to her new personal assistant. She didn't even wait until I was gone, to jump into action. I smiled to myself wickedly.

"Amber and I have to run out. Make sure you call me with the schedule and the segment lineup before any final decisions are made on what airs. I might not be back today, but I'll be available by phone," Christian instructed. The nerdy girl scribbled wildly on her legal pad and shook her head up and down so fast, it was a wonder she didn't get dizzy.

Christian turned back to me. "Khloé, I must say, I am so proud of you. Keep up the good work," she said. "Make sure you get out there and keep getting after it. We will drop your exclusives as soon as you have it all together . . . Just keep on letting me know your ideas," Christian said, squeezing my shoulder reassuringly.

I blushed. Although I knew Christian was a damn snake, it still felt good to have her compliment me for a change.

"Will do, Christian. Like you said, I learned from the best."

I was so into my conversation with Christian, it wasn't until after I was really leaving the area that I noticed Liza standing off to the side with her eyes squinted into dashes, her nostrils flaring, and her chest heaving. She turned her back just as I approached where she stood, so I don't think she saw me.

"This is *not* over. You want a fucking exclusive . . . you just wait. I'll give you a *real* exclusive. All of you will pay," Liza grumbled angrily.

Hearing her words sent a chill down my spine, but I shook it off as just the pressure we were all under at the news station to do a good job.

7

REVELATIONS

Birds chirping from the trees in the yard, the bright October sun, and the fresh green grass of the manicured lawn made the house look like an idyllic picture from *Better Homes & Gardens* magazine. It looked like a place where you'd see a father mowing the lawn, while the mother was inside baking fresh biscuits from scratch, while the daughter sat on a kitchen stool learning and the son washed the family dog at the side of the house. That was my first impression of the house that Anton Barker occupied. It wasn't too outlandish, like a mansion or anything. Instead, it was a modest house for the type of money Kyle had told me Barker was getting under the table from his crooked clients.

"He lives here?" I asked Kyle, eyeing him seriously, like maybe he was off base with his information.

Kyle let out a long sigh. He was tired of me questioning him every time he took me to another place to build my story. So far, we'd followed Detective Keith a few more times and I'd gotten pictures with my long-lens camera of him dealing directly in the street dirt. Still, every time Kyle took me someplace new, the reporter in me would be filled with doubt and ask a hundred follow-up questions to clarify. I'd tried to explain to Kyle that everything I reported on had to be verified and then verified again. Our word wasn't going to be good enough in the scheme of things.

Kyle shook his head like he didn't believe me. He'd told me before we got there that whenever Barker had to be paid off by his drug kingpin clients, someone had to hand deliver the payoff to his house. Barker wasn't taking a chance meeting anywhere else, because he was paranoid about someone taking pictures of him getting the goods.

A few times the paid delivery guy was my brother. Kyle had been all inside Barker's house dozens of times, delivering cash, jewelry, expensive show tickets, you name it, to Barker. It didn't make sense to me that a man trying to be so careful would allow anyone to know where he lives. Kyle said he'd witnessed firsthand what kind of payouts Barker, the potential future mayor of Norfolk, was taking. He'd delivered bags of cash and diamonds so flawless they'd blind an eagle.

"Look, of course he lives here. Why else would I bring you here? I told you, I been here before . . . lots of times. You thought you were going to see some big mansion? Don't you think Barker is smarter than that?" Kyle answered, turning to look at me.

I shrugged. "I just . . . It's a . . . a . . . regular-ass house," I came back. "I mean, for someone who is supposed to have so much money coming in, I just thought . . . you know something . . . um . . . nicer, bigger."

"And this house being low-key like this is the smartest shit he could do to protect himself. If the nigga was a struggling criminal defense attorney one day, and all of a sudden a mansion-buying baller the next day, he would get too much unwanted attention . . . in the streets and in society in general. You know all about Bank Secrecy laws and those suspicious-activity reports they file if a nigga bring over ten stacks into the bank in cash. Well, it's the same when buying property. If your ass can't explain where the money came from, all sorts of feds will be digging into your personal shit. That's what I was trying to tell you, twin. Anton Barker is very smart and thorough about his shit. I know he has money hidden in the walls of that house. He can't take that money to no bank, and there is but so much he can wash through his law firm. Washing money is not easy these days—the feds be on it like a hornet. I only brought you here to drive that point home, because in order to get something concrete on that nigga, you're going to have to get close to him, which is very fucking dangerous. Which is also why I will be with you every step of the way, no matter what you say. If something happened to you because of this shit, I'd be sick the rest of my life. They might as well bury me too," Kyle said, his words hitting home with me. I was touched.

"Well, I guess that settles it," I said, breathing out loudly and on the verge of tears. I don't know why I always got so emotional when my brother spoke up about me and was so adamant about protecting me. Maybe it was because I felt the same exact way about him. If something were to ever happen to him, I'd die too.

"Anyway, like you always tell me, we ain't got no time for the mushy stuff," I said, nudging Kyle's arm playfully.

"Word," he agreed, chuckling. "No mushy shit, twin."

"Now, back to this nigga," Kyle said, quickly changing the subject back to the matter at hand. "Barker got a thing for the ladies. He got a bad habit, in fact. The nigga is a sex addict, if you ask me. I heard his shit be off-the-hook wild. I feel like that is the one area he loses himself and lets down his guard. It's the one area you will have to exploit to get closer to him and the inside to see more . . . to get real pictures of him and maybe some video. Where he is all put together in everything else . . . his sex sickness is what will be the thing to bring his ass down," Kyle told me.

I shook my head, contemplating how much of my soul I was willing to sell to win over Christian and that prime spot. Barker was a good-looking man, but I wasn't ready to be fucking for a story. Maybe some flirting or whatever. The way Kyle was making it seem, I would have to be alone with him or something.

"So, what do you suggest I do?" I asked Kyle.

"You will have to get real close to him . . . a thought I don't like at all," Kyle answered. "You're real lucky I want to help you save your job, or else I wouldn't even be entertaining this cloak-and-dagger shit we been doing," Kyle continued, shaking his head back and forth. "This is a lot."

"Well, I appreciate you," I said genuinely.

"Yeah, right," he came back at me. "We already established what I said about Barker is true. He is the behind-the-scenes king of Norfolk. So you know you have to mind your p's and q's and be on high alert whenever you go under to get next to him. I know this chick who he liked to fuck. She told one of my boys, Barker is into kinky shit and he goes to great lengths to try and hide, but yet he picks up random chicks because his sex addiction is so bad. I found out that homegirl went missing, never to be found again, after somebody in the hood snitched on her and said she told people she had fucked Barker with a strap-on. So you see what I mean—on the one hand, in business he is real careful, but his true exploitation point is women and fetish sex," Kyle told me.

I was silent. What could I say to my brother after he'd just scared the living shit out of me? Silence fell between us for what seemed like an eternity. Suddenly the dark cherry-wood door, with its colorful beveled glass inserts, opened and a beautiful woman stepped out. She had a large tote bag in hand. She was dressed in a dark gray sweat suit with her hair pulled back in a sleek, loose ponytail. She was extremely beautiful, with a perfect shape. From where I sat, I could see that she had slanted eyes and clear, blemish-free skin. I bit down on my bottom lip . . . I don't know why, but I felt a pang of gnawing jealousy as if I were Barker's mistress or something. A little boy bounded out of the door, his tiny fitted cap and crisp white sneakers gleaming in the daylight. He was absolutely adorable, looking like a miniature Anton Barker. Kyle and I watched in silence. Kyle hadn't told me Barker had a family.

"So he's married too?" I asked, confused. I leaned my head back on the headrest, exasperated. This shit just kept getting deeper and more complex by the day. "How could he be into all this illegal shit, knowing he has a wife and a kid to think about? I just don't understand. He went to law school, obviously. He has all the tools to just be legit in life."

Kyle looked over at me like I was dumb. I raised my eyebrows at him to signal that he'd never told me Barker had a whole family.

"What don't you understand about everything I've been telling you these past few weeks?" Kyle asked me. He didn't give me a chance to answer before he went on. "This nigga is living a double life, twin. He's married with a kid, yet he has a sex addiction and fucks random hood chicks with reckless abandon. He's a legit criminal defense attorney to some real high-level clients, yet he is a big-time criminal who takes bribes, has people killed, and dabbles in any and everything illegal that will get him paid. I mean, like I said, a walking scandal for you," Kyle replied, then shrugged.

"Wow! You're right . . . a walking scandal," I agreed, flabbergasted by it all. "But a whole family, though? I guess these guys get into stuff and they never think about the consequences of their actions. He ain't scared to have payoffs happening at his house, where his wife and kid live? Anything could happen. Any dude could get jealous and decide to run up in there and lay them all down," I said.

"Shh," Kyle hushed me, and pointed through the windshield to turn my attention back to the house.

The beautiful woman and the little boy pulled away from the house in a sleek black BMW truck, but there was still no sign of Barker. Kyle told me we could roll out, but I didn't want to. I insisted we wait to actually see Barker and try to follow him. So we waited and waited.

"Twin, you sleep?" Kyle whispered, shaking me awake. Hours had passed since Barker's family had left the house.

"Look . . ." He jutted his chin forward, toward the house. "Finally, this dude emerges. It's about damn time."

"And here is the man himself," I whispered, my voice still gruff with sleep. "I thought he would never come out, but here he is in all his grandeur." As usual, Barker was sharply dressed. This time he didn't wear a suit, but he was still dressed nicely in a pair of dark-colored, slim-fitting slacks, a black leather jacket, and a pair of loafers that, even from a distance, I could tell were expensive.

"I know . . . my fucking back is stiff from sitting here. I got to piss too," Kyle grumbled.

"You're a trouper for sitting out here with me just for a

glimpse of this dude. At least I got a reason, you get nothing at all out of all this stuff," I said gratefully.

Kyle nodded in agreement. "You ain't never lie."

I chuckled.

The sun had already begun to set in Barker's neighborhood and the area died down and became less visible with people. I started getting nervous that someone would spot us parked a few feet away from Barker's house for that long. I knew how nosy neighbors could be, especially when they noticed strange cars or people in their quiet neighborhoods. The trees on the block gave us some cover, but I knew if we got spotted, it would be all over for Kyle and me. It was bad enough Kyle was taking this chance, knowing Barker could identify him as someone who'd delivered to him before. It was also bad that we both chose to wear all black and looked like two burglars dressed like that. All it would take is one nosy neighbor to get scared and call the cops. That would be a disaster. Not only would our cover be blown, but I'm sure they would alert Barker about us.

Another few minutes passed before Barker made any more moves. He was flanked by three men in suits. I swear, you would've thought this dude was the president the way he moved.

"He got paid security?" I asked Kyle. "Or do you not see what I'm seeing?"

"That's Norfolk PD detectives. When a person runs for office, the department assigns them a small security detail, just like how the Secret Service protects the president. But, of course, you know our friend the dirty detective made sure he had control over who was assigned. They couldn't just put any other legit cop on Barker's protective detail. He can't afford to let his dirty ways be exposed," Kyle explained.

"Our taxpayer dollars hard at work protecting damn criminals. A shame," I said.

We watched as Barker got into a darkly tinted SUV. I held my breath as the vehicle pulled out from the house.

"And we are on," Kyle said, waiting a few minutes before pulling his car out behind the vehicle transporting Barker. We carefully followed him for what seemed like forever and through a series of back roads through Virginia. My nerves were on edge every time we came to another desolate road or we turned off the main roads. I just knew they'd notice we were following them. Kyle was a smart driver, though. Some of the times he'd fall back so far, I just knew we would lose them. We never did.

Kyle and I did not speak the whole time, both of us were nervous as hell. Kyle was probably doing like me and holding his breath. We finally arrived at the place Barker was going. It was a nondescript brown building that looked kind of like a warehouse from the outside. His driver pulled the SUV through a gate that seemed to open on its own. Kyle and I had a clear view of the building. We didn't dare go through the gate to follow. We weren't that hard-pressed.

"I have no idea what this place is," Kyle finally spoke. "I've never heard of this or came out here before. This shit is sketchy-looking. I don't know about sitting out here, twin. I don't like it around here," Kyle said, leery. He let his eyes rove around and then looked over his shoulder and out of the rearview mirror.

"But look," I said, my words breaking off. Kyle turned to see what I was pointing out.

Our jaws dropped slightly at the same time. My body stiffened and my breath caught in my throat. I swallowed hard and Kyle's eyes went as round as saucers. For a few seconds neither of us said anything, we just stared at what was unfolding in front of us.

"Are those underage girls?" I gasped, sheer disbelief stringing through my words at what I was watching unfold in front of me.

"I can't be fucking seeing what I'm seeing," Kyle said. "I knew this nigga was sick, but . . ."

My mouth hung open so long, my lips turned white, while my heart hammered against my chest bone.

"Did you know he was into kids? You said he had a sex addiction, but I assumed it was with adults," I said. I was in so much disbelief, my words came out like puffs of air. "Kyle, you never said it was kids that he liked. Look at that little girl that man is practically dragging out of that van . . . she can't be more than twelve fucking years old. Oh, my God, Kyle, we got to stop this from going down. We can't just let this happen . . . Those are tiny fucking babies. There's a whole line of them. They look scared as hell being herded like cows. Nah, we got to stop it," I demanded, my voice forceful but shaky. "I don't care if it blows the story . . . we can't let this happen like this. We can't . . . I wouldn't be able to live with myself, Kyle. C'mon, we have to find a way to get out there and save them."

"Are you kidding me, twin? What the fuck we going to do? Run out there and say, 'Yo, Anton Barker, let them little girls go'?" Kyle gritted, glaring at me. "There is nothing we can do now. This shit is fucked-up, and I wasn't expecting it at all, but we have to think about our safety and be smart about this. What the fuck we going to do now? Out here with no protection, no people, and my one pistol against Barker and his bodyguards, who are all packing major heat. We are outgunned. So, what are we going to do? Nothing . . . that's what. We are here, and we can't turn back, or else everything you've been doing is over. So the only thing to do is get the pictures and prove that this nigga is a pervert. But prove it later when we have all the facts straight. We ain't running out there, yelling, 'Stop, stop!' Our lives will be fucking over, Khloé. We might as well put my gun to both our heads and pull the trigger if we do that dumb shit. It's either us or him, right now," Kyle said harshly, leaning over toward me so I could see the seriousness on his face and understand what he was saying to me, loud and clear.

"This is so wrong, Kyle. We can go out there and stop it . . . We can act like we are lost or something. We can't let innocent kids just get used up and abused like that. It's up to us to save them," I said back, just as harshly, putting my hands on both sides of my now-pounding head. "I'll get out alone and make a distraction. I'll think of something. I'll scream or call for help like someone is chasing me . . . I don't know, but I feel like I have to do something. I can't even imagine grown-ass men trafficking little-ass girls right here in our faces and we do nothing about it."

Kyle reached over and snatched me by my collar and pulled me over to him. He got in my face. He scared me with that sudden movement.

"Khloé, you can't be that fucking weak. I know you want to be noble and be a fucking hero, but you have to be smarter than this. You think this shit is just that easy? You think I feel like explaining to Mama how you got your brains blown out? Just as hard as it was to see, it's even harder to stop. We didn't plan to see these little girls in danger, I get it. But Barker is the fucking Devil. This the nigga who did unthinkable shit to people in the street and slept fine at night. What the hell? You act like you can't fucking think logically right now. Think about all the shit he will continue to do if you die before you can blow the lid off his story. This nigga out here fucking babies and goes home at night like he ain't do nothing. So you think he won't blow your ass away, wipe the blood off of his shoes, and keep it moving? Think about Mama . . . she has suffered enough after Daddy got killed. Just think!" Kyle growled, fisting my collar so tightly that his knuckles struggled against my skin.

My head swirled from a rush of adrenaline and hot, angry tears streamed down my face. I squeezed my eyes shut, fighting against invasive thoughts that trampled into my mind at that moment. I'd never told Kyle, but I was sexually abused at one of our foster homes. I was only eleven. I'd never told anyone, but seeing those girls jerked my mind right back to that hurtful place . . .

Kyle and I had been placed in yet another new foster home. In this home we had separate rooms, unlike all of the rest where we shared and could sleep together when we got scared. It was only our second week in the home, when it happened. I had just closed the door to my room and got ready for bed. I had been startled by something moving in the dark. I jumped so hard, a little bit of pee came out into my panties.

My foster father Mr. Cloy had moved out of the shadows and walked over to my bed. His dark skin made it look like it was just a set of eyes and teeth in my room. I had let out a long whimper at the sight of him. I knew he couldn't be there for anything good.

"What are you doing in my room?" I had asked sassily. "Get out," I snapped, walking backward a few steps.

Mr. Cloy walked toward me. I squinted my eyes in the darkness.

"Come over here and don't make no noise," he whispered, sounding like a snake hissing.

I folded my face into a frown and folded my arms indignantly. "No . . . you're not supposed to be in here . . ." I never got to finish my sentence.

Before I could move, run, put my hands up in defense, or do anything, that grown-ass fiftysomething-year-old man barreled into me like a bulldozer. I fell backward. My ass had hit the floor so hard, my butt ached.

"Be quiet, or I will kill you and your brother," he had growled almost inaudibly, forcing his huge hand over my nose and mouth so I couldn't scream. He held on to me roughly by my arm, and that is when I saw that he had a small knife in his other hand. My chest moved up and down like I'd just run a relay race. I couldn't catch my breath as I saw my whole life flash before my little eyes.

"Mmm," I had groaned, trying in vain to loosen his painful grip on my arm. Tears had immediately sprung to my eyes. Mr. Cloy threw me on the bed roughly. I inched away, but he grabbed my legs and pulled me toward him violently. I tried to kick him, but my little legs and feet did nothing.

"If you scream, you die," he huffed in my face. His mouth reeked of whatever he had been drinking. His entire body stank like liquor, sweat, and fried chicken.

"Ah!" I started to scream, but it was short-lived. I felt a sharp pain across my face that sent the scream tumbling right back down my throat. My eyes had shut involuntarily, and little streaks of silver lights swirled around on the inside of my eyelids. Mr. Cloy slapped me again, this time on the other side of my face. He'd hit me so hard; I saw stars. I felt buried alive because my brain was saying, *Run, fight, scream*. My body, though, wouldn't move. I couldn't breathe.

The smell of Mr. Cloy's sweaty hand filled my nostrils

as he clamped it down roughly over my nose and mouth again. I tried again to kick my legs, but his weight was too much. I had been pinned down. Pain swirled through my head so badly, I could barely open my eyes. He used one of his muscular legs to force mine apart. He was fumbling under me. Then I felt his hands moving over my private parts. I couldn't fight. I couldn't move. I couldn't breathe. There had been more erratic movement from Mr. Cloy; then I felt something slimy up against my thigh.

Mr. Cloy had started grunting hard and had started shaking like his nerves were bad. I could tell the slimy thing was in his hand now. Mr. Cloy had let out a series of sighs and animallike grunts. Then suddenly pain had filled my torso, abdomen, butt, and leg. It felt like someone had stuck a fire-lit stick into my body.

The grunts coming from Mr. Cloy are what I remember the most. He had sounded like a bull on the charge. I knew then that what had happened would change my life forever. I also knew that I would never allow it to happen again, not to me or to anyone.

I shook off my hurtful memory and opened my tear-filled eyes to look at my brother. "You don't understand, Kyle. Pieces of shit like him are always protected in society and in families and everywhere. I can't stand it," I cried.

In my pain I still couldn't bring myself to tell Kyle what had happened to me, and why I felt so strong about what we'd just found out about Anton Barker . . . the possible fucking future mayor of Norfolk.

"I know all of that, okay! But this ain't the time . . . he will get his, but this is not the time. We can't do shit right now," Kyle said, and shook his head. He slumped back in his seat and pinched the bridge of his nose like he always did whenever he was stressed-out. I knew Kyle hated when

I cried or was upset. He also hated when I showed weakness.

"I know Barker deserves to be busted up, I'm down for that, but to risk your life is not smart. You're going to jump out there, get killed, and those little girls still ain't going to get saved. You feel me," Kyle continued to press.

"I'm going to listen to you this time. But just know that I am not giving up. I am even more motivated to break this story now," I said flatly. It had taken me a few minutes to compose myself. Kyle was right: If I died trying to save those kids, then no one would ever know. I had to force myself to take the emotion out of my actions. It was a skill that took some perfecting, but I was going to have to do it if I wanted to stay alive and get this story down.

"I'm not going to let you get yourself killed, twin. I love you, and ain't nothing worth not having you around and by my side for life. If you be patient, we will take these bastards down and win you all the TV awards they got out there," Kyle said, turning to face me again.

I turned my attention back to the warehouse building and there was no real movement outside it.

"You think I can squeeze through that gate and see if I can get to a window or slip inside," I asked Kyle without looking at him.

Before he could answer, Barker and his people came outside. A few of them stood around him and he spoke, moving his hands as if he was giving instructions.

"I guess he just answered the question for you," Kyle said as we both watched the possible future mayor of our city surrounded by his minions. I could only imagine what he was telling them to do with those poor little girls locked up inside.

I shook my head in agreement and watched. The nervousness I had felt when I first saw Barker at his house and at this building had faded into a burning, vengeful hatred. Mayor or no mayor, connected or not, Anton Barker had to go down for everything that he was doing. Suddenly I couldn't keep still in my seat as I thought about the pure satisfaction I was going to get from taking him down. My chest heaved up and down as my mind raced like crazy.

You're going down. You're going down, I chanted in my head; my fists were clenched tightly. I was so riled up about it that I could feel every nerve in my body coming alive.

I watched through squinted eyes as Barker threw his head back and laughed out loud. Even his laugh from a distance sent chills down my spine.

What man who is a father would do the things he is doing to kids? I thought. *A sick bastard like him doesn't deserve a child.*

Barker finally shook hands with some of the other men there. I watched him climb into the SUV, and his three security guards did so after him. This was definitely a different side of him than I'd seen from watching him campaign and from his appearances on TV. His previous words reverberated in my head:

"Well, let's just say I am a man of the people . . . all people. I come from humble beginnings and worked my way through law school. It wasn't easy, so I understand the plight of every man, woman, and child in Norfolk. From the rich to the poor, I've been around them all. I will continue to serve the people."

I clenched my fists, infuriated at the thought of him deceiving the entire city, when he was a double-dealing criminal and child exploiter.

I followed the SUV with my eyes as the gate opened so that the vehicle could roll through. My heart throttled up in my chest as Kyle prepared to follow Barker's car; the anticipation of what was coming causing my legs to shake fiercely.

"He's going to get everything he deserves," I whispered almost breathlessly, my legs trembling now.

"All in due time, twin. All in due time," Kyle replied as we trailed the man who was going to make me a star.

8

DANGEROUS LIAISONS

After a week of more digging and running the streets, Kyle and I finally found out how Anton Barker, possibly our future mayor, got around being noticed with his sick sexual deviancies. Kyle realized that Arsenio Galina, drug dealer and a former client of Barker's, had closed off his club to let Barker have his little private parties inside. That was how Barker fulfilled his sick sex addiction and deviant proclivities without it getting out to his wife and the voting public. It was open to women, and Barker's closest clients, and their men, and that was it.

Kyle wasn't exactly part of their crew, but he'd run enough errands for some of the dudes that he was able to get in. He snuck me in through the back. He'd told me I would have to dress like the women Barker liked and I'd have to play along. He'd found out that the parties could get wild, with the men really coming on to the women strongly. I was ready. Whatever it took to get this last piece of evidence to blow the lid off Barker and his bullshit, I'd do it. It wasn't like I hadn't put myself in many dangerous situations for stories thus far.

I snuck into the bathroom first, after Kyle opened the back door. I slipped into a stall, took off the trench coat I'd been wearing, and slipped into the heels I had in my bag. I left the stall, pushed my stuff down into the trash can, and hooked myself up in the mirror. I must say, I hadn't looked that sexy in a long while. I'd been so busy working that I had forgotten how pretty my butter-colored skin could be up against my hazel eyes. My hair had been in a ponytail for so long, I had not realized how beautiful and long it was now. I shook my head at myself. *Work, work, work. That's all I've been doing lately. Chasing that spot on TV.*

I hadn't had time to date or go out with friends, or even spend any quality time with my mother and Kyle. All of the time I'd been spending with Kyle lately had been chasing this story. I stared at myself for a few seconds, wondering whether or not selling my soul for a story was worth it anymore. I'd sacrificed a lot.

The music reverberated off the walls of Club Pulse and thumped through my body. I'd never been a club girl. I always hated real loud music, and now was no different. Still, I would deal with it for a good reason.

Sitting alone at the bar, I looked out into the club as the carefully placed partygoers moved their hips to the music—a few of them looked like they needed to be in a music video.

Kyle had told me that I needed to give off the vibe that I belonged there. To fit in with the other beautiful women Barker had chosen, I had let my hair loose and it fell in sandy coils down my back. I dressed in a shocking hot-pink, formfitting dress that accentuated all of the booty I had inherited from my mother, a pair of heels that made me look model tall, and a full face of makeup that was so different for me. The bartender turned toward me and without another word set a drink in front of me. I found that odd, but I guessed that everything inside this private party was controlled. Playing my role, I smiled coyly at the bartender and picked up the drink.

I nursed the shit out of that drink, pretending that I was drinking it. I had no idea what type of shit they might've put in the drink, so I wasn't taking a chance. I turned from the bar and took in the sights of the club. Namely, my mark—Anton Barker—who was, of course, surrounded by throngs of women and a phalanx of men and security.

What I was learning is that our wannabe mayor was a sophisticated, two-faced bastard of a criminal. Anton Barker had defended and now worked for the drug cartels behind the scene. I knew if he became mayor, our little city was going to blow up with crime. Adding to that, to know he was into exploiting children sexually and more than likely trafficking them, made it even worse in my eyes. I watched Barker from afar for a while, but I knew I couldn't get all of the information I needed from that far away. Kyle had lingered around, but then one of the bosses had sent him on an errand. Had he refused, he would've brought suspicion on himself. He'd given me the eye that said, *Be fucking careful and be smart.* I had nodded, letting him know I understood.

After a little while at the bar, I decided it was time for me to try and get a little closer. I wanted to hear Barker's voice, watch his movements, and look into his eyes. I jumped down from the bar stool I had been holding down and suddenly felt a tight grasp on my elbow. My body stiffened and I clutched my purse, where I had one of my father's old knives sandwiched between two maxi pads—which is how Kyle told me to hide it, just in case Barker sent his men around to search the girls they allowed inside to party. I rounded on the person touching me and wore a scowl on my face that said, *I'm not with the shits.*

"I was just going to ask if I could get you another drink,

since you didn't drink that one," the man said, quickly letting me go when he saw the angry scowl on my face.

A flash of heat came over me. He had obviously been watching me. And why was he being so polite? Weren't all the women there to be used at Barker's request?

"You shouldn't touch someone like that," I spat, shooting daggers at him with my eyes. "A simple 'Can I get you a drink?' might've gotten you somewhere," I hissed.

Although my nostrils flared, and my left hand had curled into a fist on its own, I couldn't help but notice how fine the stranger was. His skin was smooth like newly melted caramel, his round eyes were adorned by the thickest, longest lashes I'd ever seen on a man, and the dark, tight curls hugging his head were perfectly cut and lined up. He was also dressed nicely.

"I usually don't approach women in situations like this," the gorgeous stranger said. "But you're beautiful, and my boss wants to meet you. I'm just the messenger—don't shoot the messenger," he said.

A flash of shame and embarrassment lit my cheeks aflame. I shifted my weight from one foot to the other and broke eye contact with the man. It wasn't often I was told I was beautiful, and my brain immediately flew into defensive mode. The last time I'd heard I was beautiful, it had been from my ex, right before my phone blew up with a bitch he had been fucking the whole time we'd been together. I didn't take that compliment too well.

"Who is your boss? Looks like a lot of bosses in here," I said, then turned away to look out into the crowd for emphasis of my point. As soon as I turned around, I could feel the heat of someone's hard gaze on me. *Oh, shit!* I screamed in my head. It was Barker . . . staring right at me. I was immediately unnerved, but I had to play it cool. This was a matter of life or death at that point.

"Follow me and I'll show you who my boss is," the man said, moving away from the bar and getting in front of me so I could follow him.

I inhaled deeply as we made our way to an area of the club that was closer to the VIP section. I took a seat where I could still see Barker partying. Women surrounded him as he took in the attention like he needed it to breathe. He laughed as the women scrambled around him like paid entertainers. A vision of Barker's wife flashed through my mind, then his beautiful little boy, and lastly I saw those little girls that had been herded out of a truck at that warehouse. My jaw rocked, but I kept a partial smile on my face. I knew I needed to look friendly or I might get my ass tossed out of this private party.

"You, I want you," Barker slurred, pointing to a tall, slim, muscular girl standing right next to me. My shoulders slumped with relief. I wanted to be close, but not so close that this nasty bastard had to touch me the way he was touching those women. I watched the slim girl rush over and put her breasts in Barker's face, and then a man walked over, dumped a small mound of cocaine on the table, and grabbed the girl's hair and made her snort it. Barker threw his head back and laughed.

"My kind of woman!" he yelled. Then the same man forced the girl's head from the table into Barker's crotch. Loud laughter followed.

I watched as the girls around Barker were forced to snort lines of cocaine and chase it down with shot after shot of Patrón. By the time the VIP section was almost cleared out, most of them could hardly stand. Barker and the girl he'd chosen were fondling and licking each other as his people tried to urge him to leave.

"I'm the fucking boss. I'm going to be the mayor. I say when it's time," Barker slurred.

I hadn't seen him take drugs, but he'd certainly had his fill of drinks. I'd been dying to take out my cell phone to get pictures, but it was too risky. I knew I was being watched. If the security wasn't so deep, I could've taken the pictures right then, but I decided to wait. I wasn't giving up until I got something from this undercover mission.

I looked at my cell phone clock. It was already three o'clock in the morning. I remembered Kyle saying that when Barker had these private parties, he usually opted to stay downtown at the posh Crowne Plaza hotel for more wild partying and to scratch that sexual itch of his. As Barker prepared to leave, the girls he hadn't chosen were herded out the door. Basically, kicked out. I prepared to join the herd, when the guy that had approached me earlier grabbed my arm again.

"Hey," he said, holding on to me.

I whipped my head toward him. "You just don't learn, huh?" I asked, annoyed.

"You've been picked for the after party," he said.

My heart started pounding. The first thing I thought about was Kyle not being there with me and not knowing where I would be.

"Is that how this works? He picks who he wants," I asked.

"Yeah, and we just do what he asks," he said, shrugging. Something in his eyes told me he wasn't down for the bullshit Barker was doing, but he worked within this shit and had to comply or die.

This guy was sweet on me. I could tell. Right away I thought he might be a good source of more information to use for my story.

"I guess I have no choice," I replied. And I really didn't. If I wanted the real dirt, I was going to have to go along with whatever came my way.

"Not really," the guy said. He led me toward where a different group of women was standing. As we walked, I figured I'd probe him and see how far I could get. If he even answered one question, I would know I had him. If he told me to shut the fuck up, I would know I was in big damn trouble and about to see and do God knows what to get this story.

"What's your name?" I asked the guy, batting my eyelashes this time. I might as well have played along to get what I want.

"Dee," he answered vaguely, as if he had just come up with that off the dome.

"Nice to meet you, Dee," I said.

"And yours?" he asked.

"Kay," I returned with a vague response of my own. I was cheering for myself silently. He'd not only answered my question, but he'd shown me he was interested. That was all I needed.

9

ON A MISSION

We left the club and headed to the hotel. The women being transported with me in the Mercedes Sprinter minibus were all in different stages of intoxication. The scent of sweat, perfume, ass, and weed made for a bad mix of odors wafting around the vehicle. I was out of my league, for sure. These chicks obviously sold ass for a living. Who else would allow themselves to be herded around like cattle going to slaughter? It would take some skill for me to remain calm when I got close to Barker. I'd been in real sketchy undercover roles as a reporter before, but I was confident in my abilities. We were loaded out of the vehicle a couple at a time. Dee, my new friend, made sure I was in the group of girls following him.

"Good evening," Dee said to the concierge behind the desk at the hotel. The man nodded and smiled politely, like he was very familiar with Dee.

"You know who sent me. He's had a wild night and wants me to prepare the rooms," Dee said, sounding official. The man behind the desk made a face that read as a mixture of understanding and disgust at the same time.

"You know how it can get, so make sure you secure the entire floor. It can get very wild," Dee said, using his hands to depict a sexual act. "No one we don't know is to come up to that floor at all. You know the drill, but I was told to repeat it. Absolutely imperative that you secure the adjoining rooms and everything," Dee said, sliding money across the counter in the man's direction.

I furtively snapped a picture with my cell phone. This was solid proof of Barker having his people pay off others to keep their secrets.

"Yes." The man smiled, quickly placing his hand on top of the cash and sliding it off the counter. "The usual?" he asked.

"Of course," Dee said. He picked up a stack of card keys, spoke to another guy standing by, and then had us all head for the elevators.

When we got upstairs, a few of us were taken into a suite where there was music playing and the party continued.

"So, what happens now?" I asked Dee as I boldly walked over to him.

"You can wait and see," he answered stoically. All of a sudden his mood changed. I walked away as more men filed in and out of the room. They partied with girls and some took them and left.

Almost an hour later, Barker and his companion entered the suite. A rush of excitement and nervousness flooded my body, causing my skin to feel tingly and sensitive. I followed them with my eyes and read Barker's mouth as he told one of the guys he was going to the room next door. With the extra key I grabbed from the table next to the lamp, I quickly slipped out before Dee noticed and anyone else could miss me—or at least I hoped they didn't.

I got inside the other room and hid in the bathroom, pulling the shower curtain closed as I stepped into the tub. I heard when Barker came inside with the same slim, big-busted girl from the club. I listened to the sound of smacking and sucking and pictured Barker and the girl from the club tongue kissing and fondling each other.

"Let me go freshen up," I heard the girl say to Barker.

"Hurry up!" I heard him reply, sounding like he wasn't happy.

My heart raced as I heard the girl step into the bathroom and lock the door. I peeked out from a small opening in the pulled shower curtain and watched the girl undress. Just like I had suspected, her breasts were huge, unnatural-looking implants, but as I watched the girl finish undressing, something else happened that I didn't expect. The door opened and a little girl walked inside.

Oh, shit! I cupped my hands over my mouth and watched the slim girl grab the little girl through the doorway.

I shook my head. *These motherfuckers are sick!*

"What does he want you to do?" the slim girl asked the little girl, who couldn't be any more than thirteen years old. The little girl shrugged.

"They gave me this," she said, holding up a flimsy piece of lace lingerie.

The slim girl shook her head in disgust. "Nasty motherfuckers. Just know I am not okay with this," she whispered to the little girl. Then she went about helping the little girl dress up to look more like a grown woman. While I watched, I gripped my father's hunting knife in my bag until my knuckles paled. I felt all kinds of emotions swirling around me like hurricane-force winds. I thought about Kyle's warnings and I knew I was trapped and had to be quiet. I was there to get pictures and information. I was there to get evidence. I was there to bring down the would-be mayor who'd proven himself to be a disgusting piece of shit. I had a brand-new resolve inside me. I was ready.

The blonde went into her purse and retrieved a small glassine envelope of cocaine, dumped a tiny mound onto the back of her hand, and inhaled deeply.

"Ah! I'm going to need this to fuck this nasty old motherfucker," the slim girl whispered. "You should take one too. It'll make it easier to cope," she said to the little girl.

That made me furious. I went to pull back that curtain and stop that baby from taking those drugs, but then . . .

"Aye! C'mon! I don't have all night!"

The slim girl, the little girl, and I all jumped when Barker banged on the bathroom door and started yelling for them to hurry up.

"I'm coming!" the slim girl called out in a fake, flirty voice.

"Shut the fuck up and wait," the slim girl grumbled quietly, grabbing the shower curtain and yanking it back. Her eyes popped open and her mouth dropped open into a wide O. She was so shocked to see me, a scream got stuck and wouldn't come out.

"Shh," I warned, putting the point of my knife out in front of me.

The girl closed her eyes and swallowed hard. Tears immediately drained from the corners of her eyes. The little girl covered her mouth with her hands.

"Don't scream. I'm going to help you," I whispered to the little girl.

"I have nothing to do with his business. I'm not the one you want. I just get paid to be here," the slim girl whispered.

"You need to go out there and distract him so I can get this little girl out of here," I whispered back harshly, pushing the knife into the slim girl's skin just before it was enough to draw any blood. "Put this in the room with you somewhere. I need to make sure I have this on tape," I said to her, sliding a tiny pin camera to her. She nodded her head up and down vigorously in agreement. She had no idea who I was and was probably thinking she'd just stepped into an episode of *The Twilight Zone.*

I motioned with my head for her to leave before Barker came busting in there. I was thanking God a million times in my head that the bathroom of the suite was closer to the exit than anything, and the bedroom part had a door.

The slim girl did as she was told. I reached over and turned the shower on so that Barker wouldn't hear anything when the little girl and I made our escape. I made her put on my jacket over that lingerie, which was ten times too big for her underdeveloped body. I stopped the slim girl right before she left the bathroom.

"How many men came up here with him?" I whispered.

The slim girl shrugged her shoulders.

I got closer to her and squinted my eyes. "Don't be coy now. I am trying to help us all get out of here alive. I won't leave you for dead," I huffed in her face.

"Fuck," she panted, wiping the sweat off of her head. "You must not know how dangerous these people are. You think I want to be here? If I could just run, I would have already," she whispered harshly.

"I'll ask you again—how many men are out there?" I whispered through clenched teeth as I held the knife perilously close to the slim girl's throat.

"They're all in the adjoining rooms. He wanted to be alone with me and her," the girl sobbed. "Nobody knows about his . . . um . . . secret," she said, darting her eyes to the little girl cowering in the corner. "So he . . . um . . . doesn't allow them in the suite with us. They are all fucked-up drunk and high and probably sleep or are fucking some of the whores he keeps around. He was supposed to be here for the night. They said they did a sweep before we came up here," the slim girl relayed. "Please, just get her out of here safely. Don't worry about me, I really hate that he makes me bring kids into the bed. It's . . . it's not my thing and I think he's disgusting," she cried.

"I will get her out and I'll make sure I meet up with you to get that video. Give me your name and number," I said, pushing my cell phone forward.

"I'm Shara," she said with a drag of sadness in her tone. "I have to go. You're saving her, but I'll have to deal with this sick bastard and his shit if I don't get out there now."

"Get out here!" Barker boomed from somewhere on the other side of the door.

I stepped back and watched as Shara exhaled, shook off her fear, and stepped out into the room. I heard her talking to Barker, saying the little girl had to use the bathroom and urging him into the bedroom until the little girl was ready. That had been good thinking on her part. I had a good feeling about Shara. She might be useful to me as an eyewitness for my news story later.

I reached out my hand toward the little girl and she grabbed mine. She was shaking all over. But, shit, so was I. "Scared" was an understatement to describe what I was experiencing at that moment. I was somewhere between being completely and utterly terrified and falling into a damn coma. Judging from the time my father was shot in front of me, I think this one takes the top spot, which means that I've never been this frightened in my life.

I pulled myself together and opened the bathroom door a crack. I could see that most of the suite was dark but for a tiny sliver of light coming from the bedroom. I yanked the door all the way this time and tugged on the little girl to follow me. It was time for us to make a run for it. At first, the tiny, trembling girl just stood there. I shot her a serious look and moved my face close to hers so I could speak so that she understood the seriousness in my tone.

"You have to come on. We will have to run," I whispered harshly. "We don't have time to play around." I took her by the hand and roughly tugged her harder this time.

"If you don't come on now, I'll leave you here and he will rape you. Do you understand that?" I said through my teeth. That finally spurred the little girl into action and she started to move right along with me. She better had, because if not, all of this risky business would've been for nothing.

When we stepped out of the bathroom into the suite, the room was dark, but I could still see the objects from the light poles outside of the parking lot. I hesitated a few seconds, letting my eyes adjust to the poorly lit room. In the room I could hear loud music coming from the room next door and something like wrestling sounds coming from the suite bedroom. That made me think of Shara and what sick shit she might be enduring at the hands of Barker. I could tell that he was an over-the-top pervert. *Fucking bastard!* I couldn't wait to expose his ass.

I shook off the thoughts that might've made me bust up in that bedroom part of the suite and kick his ass to save Shara from his shit. I craned my neck and squinted until I could see a clear path to the door. I used my fingers and hands to make signals to the little girl to tell her that we were going to the door, so she knew to follow me closely. She nodded her head like she was ready. I carefully inched to the door, slowly twisted the doorknob, and opened the door a crack. I didn't see anyone standing right outside the door, but that didn't mean there weren't guards somewhere in the vicinity. I knew better than to think Barker would be in the suite without security on tap somewhere close. I couldn't stay in the room, so I'd have to take the chance. A flash of panic lit in my chest and almost made me freeze in place, like I usually did when I was stressed-out like this.

C'mon, Khloé, you can do this. You have been through worse and gotten out of it. This is to save you and this baby. You can't get weak now. You're better than that. You got this. You got this. I gave myself a strict pep talk silently in my head.

Slowly and quietly I moved with the sneakiness of a sly fox. When I got into the hallway, I signaled the little girl to move fast. I dragged her along so fast that her feet were barely hitting the floor before she was being pulled. We both moved like two tiny gazelles. My breath came out of my mouth in raggedy, jagged puffs. I whipped my head from side to side frantically. This hallway seemed to be miles long. *What the fuck?* I cussed to myself. I couldn't see one damn door for us to run through to get to the steps. I knew getting on the elevator was a no-no. That would be like walking right into a trap. Besides, we had no time to stand and wait for an elevator. And my best guess was that Barker would have several men posted up by the elevators, just in case anyone got wind of him being in the hotel and tried to come on his floor for a quick photo opportunity, or, worse, do like me and get an entire news story on his ass.

Just as the little girl and I almost cleared the hallway, I almost lost my heart through my mouth. The little girl sucked in her breath so hard, it sounded like a round of hiccups.

"Hey! You!" a man's booming voice called after us. "Hey! Girl! Where are you going?" he yelled, standing still at the opposite end of the hallway. He must've thought we were those programmed bitches they had in those rooms, and that we would just stop at his commands. He thought fucking wrong.

"Come on. We have to run," I grunted, frantically jerking the little girl along. "We can't stop! Keep moving!"

"Bitch! Stop! Stop!" the man yelled after us, finally moving his feet to chase us. I guess it finally registered with him that we were not going to listen to his ass. Even with the terror squeezing all of my organs inside, I lifted my legs up and down, up and down, and kept it moving. I hadn't run track in high school, for nothing. If it wasn't for that little girl, I would've been even faster. I finally saw a door that led to a stairwell. I hit the door so hard, it slammed open and hit the wall with a loud bang. After busting through the door, we hit the steps. The little girl was keeping pace with me too. It must've been the fear moving us down those steps like true athletes. Within seconds I heard the door slam above us. I knew the man had entered the stairwell and was hot on our heels. I could hear his stampeding footfalls coming behind us. With every stomp my heart dropped lower and lower into my stomach.

We weren't going to make it all the way to the bottom. The man was gaining on us and I could tell the little girl was getting tired. Barker was smart. He'd had us put on a high floor for this same reason. He wanted to make sure if anyone slipped away, it would take forever to get to the bottom and out of the hotel. I can't front, Barker and his people were pretty thorough with their shit. But, still, they weren't smarter or sharper than me.

"Follow me. C'mon," I puffed out, barely able to catch my breath, much less speak. I must say, she was staying in step with me, one for one. We spiraled down the stairs at a rate so fast, it was a wonder we didn't go tumbling down. I couldn't even feel my damn legs, I swear.

"Don't make me shoot you, bitches! You better stop! Stop, I said!" the man huffed.

He was losing his wind, I could tell. He was no match for the two of us with the movement. That's because he was big like a bear and that fat belly was a hindrance to him moving that fast.

I decided to take a chance. We weren't going to make it outside, but I had to make sure we got away. By the time we got to the fifth floor, I busted into the door that led to the hallway where all of the rooms were. I started yelling at the top of my lungs.

"Help! Help us! Please! Anyone!" I screamed as we ran down another long, never-ending hallway.

I knew the dude working for Barker and his people wasn't going to keep pursuing us, because that would've brought too much attention to them and ultimately to him.

"Come this way," I huffed, pulling the little girl into the little room with the ice machine and vending machines. She was crying hysterically; her face was a messy mixture of tears and the very adult makeup the slim girl had put on her in the bathroom.

"We are going to die," the little girl cried. She was trembling so hard, she could barely stand straight. "I don't want to die. My mother is in El Salvador. She won't know if I die!"

"Shh, think positive. I'm going to get us out of here," I told her. "You just have to follow my lead, okay?" I said, trying my best to calm her down, although my whole body was shaking too.

I texted Kyle to tell him I was leaving the hotel and for him not to come there, no matter what. I didn't tell him what was really going on; if I did, I knew he'd come running there.

I grabbed the little girl and gave her strict instructions on how she needed to act. She nodded in understanding. We carefully left out of the room we'd been hiding in and I tapped on the first door next to it. I looked at its number, 511, and prayed that today it would be my lucky number. With my heart jamming against my chest wall, I said a silent prayer. Finally, an older woman opened the door. Her face immediately fell into a frown.

"Can I help you?" she grumbled, looking from me to the little girl and back again.

"We are in trouble. There are some very dangerous men upstairs that are after us, but they won't come to this floor," I blurted, moving uneasily on my legs. "Please let us in. Please," I begged.

The woman looked hesitant, but then the little girl piped up. "Please! She saved me. He . . . he was going to rape me," she cried. Her words looked like they'd sent a bolt of electricity through the lady and she quickly let us inside her room.

She pointed to the small sofa and table inside. "Um, m-make yourselves comfortable," she stammered. I could tell the woman didn't know what the hell to think, say, or do.

"I know this seems crazy, but I'm a reporter," I explained. "I went undercover for a story and I found this little girl being exploited. We made a run for it," I said, trying to tell her enough, but not too much.

The woman clutched her chest and widened her eyes. "Oh, my goodness," she gasped. "You poor little child. What can I do to help?" she asked.

My mind was racing, but I knew the first thing I had to do was get the hell out of the area.

"Do you have a car?" I asked.

"I do," she replied.

"Can you drive us away from here? I just need to get as far away with this little girl as possible. These men are dangerous and they're not going to stop pursuing us now," I said, the words falling out of my mouth at rapid speed.

"Why don't we just call the police?" the woman asked, reaching over for her cell phone.

"No! Please!" I blurted, almost rushing into her to keep her from calling 911.

She looked at me like I was out of my mind. I could see suspicion creeping back into the features of her face.

I let out an exasperated breath. "I know how this seems. Trust me, it's the stuff movies are made of, but these same men have police on their payroll. If you call, I'm afraid some of the dirty cops will show up and we will be handed right back over to the men who want to kill us. It's complicated, but I can't risk it," I told her.

"Oh . . . um . . . okay. But how will we get out?" she asked, her nerves showing in her shaky words.

"Do you have clothes we can use?" I asked. "We can put on disguises and calmly walk out to your car," I suggested.

I could actually see the fear dancing in the woman's

eyes. She paced a bit with her hands on her hips. "How in the hell did I end up in the middle of something so crazy?" She suddenly chuckled, but I could tell she didn't find anything funny at all.

"Maybe God had you open up the door for us. You were meant to save us today," I said.

The woman walked over to the window and peeked out of the curtains. She quickly put the curtain back in place.

"What do you see?" I asked.

"There are men out there walking around like they're looking for something. They're looking for you two," she replied.

I walked over to the window and peeked for myself. She was right. There were two or three guys roaming around. Barker's motorcade cars were still out there too.

"Maybe we can just wait them out," I suggested.

"I have to check out in a few hours," the woman replied.

"Shit," I huffed. Now I was pacing. I had to think. There was no way for us to make it outside without those dudes forcefully stopping us to take a look at us. But, on the other hand, the sun had come up on Barker's little perverted activity, so I knew they wouldn't be there for long. They'd be scouring the streets for an unknown girl with hazel eyes and sandy hair and a little girl, but at least we'd still be alive. At least until I could get to Shara and get the video, put it together with the material Kyle and I had amassed thus far, get to the studio safely, and then force Christian to break the story right away.

Shit! Just thinking about all I would have to do had exhausted me.

I went to open my mouth, but loud knocks on the room door startled us. The little girl jumped to her feet; her eyes were wide. I whirled around and stared at the door. The woman covered her mouth with her hand and looked at me with flared nostrils.

"Housekeeping!"

All of our shoulders seemed to relax at the same time. I breathed out loudly.

"No, thank you," the woman yelled out without opening the door. "I . . . I . . . have to get you-all out of here. This is not good for my nerves." The woman was panting; sweat dripped down the sides of her face.

"Can you call and get a later checkout?" I asked, biting the hell out of my nails. I had to do something before this woman just got sick of being scared and pushed us out of her room—or, worse, called the police on us.

"Yes. Yes. That's a perfect idea," she said, rushing her words out.

We were able to buy two more hours of time. Just like I suspected, Barker and his caravan left, but he left two guys behind to look for us. There was no choice left: We were going to have to dress in disguises and leave.

"I will definitely repay you," I told the lady as I put one of her scarves around my head and changed out of my tight dress into an old-lady walking suit she'd given me.

"I don't need anything except to get out of this alive," she said, shaking her head.

I dressed the little girl in different clothes provided by the lady too. We turned the shirt into a dress by adding a belt to it because it would've looked obvious if we tried to leave it as a shirt and added pants to it. We were also given another printed scarf, so we made it work since, they were all we had at that moment.

I looked at myself and the girl from every angle. We definitely looked totally different than we had when we'd run from Barker's room. My heartbeat sped up from the possibility of us getting caught, but equally from the potential of us getting away and me reporting on the biggest story of my life.

"Are you ready to do this?" I asked after we were all in disguise.

"Oh, my God, I'm ready, but I will say that I am terrified," the woman said honestly.

"I'm ready," the little girl spoke up. One of the rare times she'd said anything.

"All we have to do is follow the plan. I will hold on to you like you're my mother or grandmother and she will hold on to me. We have to walk fast and get to your car before any one of those dudes can think anything of seeing us—got it?" I prattled off, going over the plan I had come up with one more time to be sure. The woman and the little girl both nodded their agreement and followed me with their eyes as I paced and spoke. I looked at my cell phone. It was already heading toward noon. I hadn't answered Kyle's calls, so I knew he was probably worried sick and was going to be furious with me. I just couldn't take the chance that he would come running there and get himself into danger. I also couldn't risk anything messing up the story. I was so close to blowing the lid off Anton Barker, Detective Keith, and all of their criminal cronies. I could almost taste the satisfaction I would feel when I watched them marched out on TV in handcuffs. I just could not wait. But first, I needed to get the hell out of that hotel alive.

"Okay, then. Let's go," I said, looking around one last time.

We all followed the plan. I was a little shocked at how well the woman helping us played her role. She bent her back and walked as if she needed assistance. With my eyes covered in shades and a scarf covering my hair, I held her up and escorted her through the lobby. The little girl held on to my other arm so tightly, our pulses were almost synced. We were almost to the door leading to outside when a man's voice from behind called out.

"Miss! Miss!"

We all froze for a second. I was too afraid to turn around. The woman was too. I held my breath. My head immediately began to pound. The woman slowly turned around.

"You dropped this," the strange man said, extending a room key toward the woman.

She smiled and nodded. "Oh, thank you," she said, taking the key.

Boy was that a close call. Thank God hotel guests don't get penalized for taking hotel card keys with them because I was not going to let her go back in the hotel to return it.

Either way, that was our signal to beat feet to the car. We picked up our pace and finally made it to the woman's car. I helped her into the driver's seat for good measure, and just in case eyes were watching us. The little girl climbed into the back. I rushed around the front of the car, and just as I was about to sit down in the passenger seat, I heard it.

"Yo! I think that's her! The girl that ran!"

I felt like everything was spinning around me and I could no longer control my breathing.

"Aye! You!"

I slammed my body into the car. "Drive! Get out of here! Drive!" I screamed at the woman.

"Oh, my God!" she screamed, throwing the car into reverse and hitting the gas pedal hard. The car lurched backward as the two ran up on it, guns drawn.

"Agh!" the little girl screamed.

"Drive!" I hollered again. "Drive!" Even from where I sat, I could see the shock registering on the lady's face and in her voice.

"I'm driving, gotdammit!" she screamed.

"Fuck," I gasped, gripping the door so hard my hands hurt.

I heard the first gunshots ring out and hit the taillight on the woman's car.

"Oh, shit!" I belted out.

The woman had the gas pedal to the floor and finally we were out of the parking lot. Those dudes still had to run to their car.

"Turn left!" I screamed at her. I did that several more times until we were far enough away to slow down. I couldn't afford for us to get stopped by the police and have any of Barker's people alerted.

Once we lost the goons, the woman drove me home. I thanked her and asked for her contact information. She wasn't comfortable giving it to me, so I gave her mine.

"You'll see me on TV soon. Just know that you helped me big-time," I told her. I took the little girl inside my apartment with me. I told her to make herself comfortable. I rushed into my master bathroom and fell to my knees in front of the toilet. My body bucked and I wheezed as the hot, acidy vomit spewed out of my mouth. When it was all out, I fell back onto my butt. I closed my eyes and pressed the balls of my hands into my eyes. I hadn't even realized how hard I was crying. I lay on the floor and turned onto my side and sobbed hysterically. Seeing my life flash before my eyes, yet again, was physically, mentally, and emotionally draining. It was a while before I was able to get up and gather myself. I walked to the mirror over the sink and splashed water on my face.

I knew the message would be sent to Anton Barker that I had taken one of his exploited children. She was now the person who had firsthand knowledge of what was going on behind the scenes with Barker, which would cause a chain reaction that, I hoped, would hit Barker directly. I knew, though, this would also drag me and her right into the middle of it. Although I wanted this story really badly, I was seriously considering how much of my soul I was willing to sell for success.

10

CASUALTIES

"*B*itch! *Open this door!" I heard the deep voice, loud banging, and then deafening kicking on my door. My heart sank into the pit of my stomach. A hot flash came over my body at the sound of his voice—the familiar voice.*

"You're going to die! You messed with the wrong nigga!" the voice boomed again.

I moved around and around in circles, not knowing whether to go left or right. I didn't know how they had found me, but here I was . . . trapped. I planned to be the fuck out of Dodge before Barker and his people could get wind of my deeds.

"Open this door!" the man's voice boomed again, more angry urgency in it this time. He started banging even harder and jiggling with the doorknob. "Bitch! I'm about to take this door down and you'll be sorry!" the man barked. "You

crossed the wrong motherfucker. You wanted to sell your soul to the Devil—well, here I am!"

This time I could hear something heavy hitting up against the door.

I slid down to the floor, nowhere to run, nowhere to hide. I started praying to God to give my mother and Kyle peace if I died.

Wham!

"Oh, my God!" I blurted out when I heard the front door slam open with a clang.

I jumped out of my sleep covered in sweat. I whipped my head around and touched myself to make sure I had been dreaming and that no one was really coming through my door to get me. My chest was pumping up and down and my head pounded from jumping up out of my sleep like that. As my eyes adjusted in the dark, that's when I heard it. There was actual pounding on my door happening, just like in my dream. No wonder I was having that crazy-ass dream.

My brother was outside my door, banging like he didn't have any good damn sense. "Khloé! Open this door now!" I heard Kyle barking from the other side of the door. He pounded the door like someone was chasing him.

I frantically shrugged into my robe and raced through the apartment. The little girl, who had been sleeping on my couch, was sitting up with the blanket pulled up to her eyes. She looked terrified. She darted her eyes from me to the door and back again. I could tell she was probably already traumatized from being forced into damn sex trafficking. I walked over to her, bent down by the couch, and touched her arm.

"Don't be scared, okay. It's just my brother. He's not going to hurt you or do anything to you or me. He loves

me and is probably a little upset with me for what happened. I can handle him. Trust me, I'm not scared of him,"
I comforted, smiling afterward. She seemed to calm down
a little bit, but I could still feel her trembling slightly. That
was to be expected, I guess. She'd been through a lot.

I turned my attention back to the door. In my assessment
there was no reason for Kyle to be carrying on like that, unless his ass was on fire or he had a gun to his fucking head.
He was scaring me with the way he was carrying on.

"Open the door!" Kyle screamed again. I was shaking
all over. Between my dream, which had shaken me up
completely, and now Kyle's booming voice, I was a mess. I
could tell he wasn't fucking around—either that or he was
being chased.

"Shit!" I whispered as I started for the door, then stopped
and contemplated hiding the little girl. I whirled around
aimlessly, but soon realized that there was no time because
Kyle would probably storm through my place to look
around anyway. I didn't know what exactly he had heard,
but I knew he was pissed at me. There was nowhere for
me to go but to that door and face it. There was nowhere
for me to send the little girl either. I had only one choice,
and that was to let my brother in and deal with his wrath.
It wasn't like he hadn't been mad at me before.

"Fuck! Fuck! Fuck!" I cursed as I saw my time running
out. I knew I had no wins. Although it was my apartment,
there was no way I would be able to keep my brother's ass
out. I spun around and around some more, trying to get
my thoughts together before I let him inside. I started for-
mulating a story in my head about what I would tell him
about what happened at the club, but I was officially out
of time. Kyle was banging like a madman and he wasn't
going to go away easily. Finally I threw the door open and

met a snarling, huffing-and-puffing Kyle. He stormed into my apartment like a figurative tornado.

"Yo! Are you fucking crazy? Didn't I tell you, you had to play the role and be fucking smart if we were going to do this story shit?" Kyle roared, his accusatory pointer-finger out in front of him. He was up on me and in my face within seconds. "Didn't I warn you not to try to play fucking hero out here and just go with the fucking flow?"

I stood defenseless as he advanced on me so fast, I didn't even have time to react. I threw my hands up and backed up, inch by inch. "Kyle . . ."

He lunged forward and grabbed for my robe collar, but I sidestepped him. I knew he was mad, but he wasn't going to grab me up and treat me like I was his child this time, as he'd done many times before when he didn't agree with something I'd done.

"Kyle, wait," I said in a commanding voice as he walked me down.

"What, Khloé! What could you possibly want to explain to me! I told you, if you ever fucked with those dudes, we would be in big fucking trouble!" he snarled. "And so said, so fucking done! You are officially a wanted woman, so if that was the fucking goal you had in mind, you have fucking succeeded!"

Tears immediately rushed to my eyes and cascaded down my face as I saw the sheer hurt and disappointment in my brother's eyes.

"Ain't no use in crying now. You should've thought about that shit before you wanted to go and play fucking *Big Hero 6,*" Kyle said, finally standing still after I backed all the way up to the wall. I kept my back against the wall as he started pacing angrily in front of me. "Do you know what you have done? Huh? Can you fucking even start to

get out of that fucking fake-news world you live in inside
your head and get back to reality? They are fucking looking for you, Khloé! It will not be long before they find out
you're my sister and that I was the one who let you inside
the club that night. They are looking for the girl too,"
Kyle said, stopping for a second to look over at her. "You
fucking took a whole human being? Who does this?" Kyle
went on, shaking his head and grunting in sheer disgust.

"Well, I couldn't stand by and let that motherfucker
rape and use and abuse this baby!" I finally piped up and
defended myself. I was tired of Kyle being angry and carrying on like I didn't have a reason for what I'd done.
"You weren't there! You didn't see what I saw, Kyle! He
actually had a girl put adult lingerie on this little girl, who
barely has breasts! What the fuck you expected me to do?
Just stand in the same room and listen to this child scream
her head off while he fucked her?" I said in one big breath.

I tried to continue my justification for what I'd done,
but Kyle wasn't hearing it. Every time I opened my mouth
to go on with my reasoning and my plan going forward,
he'd put up his hand and rant some more.

"You know what the fuck I had to witness behind your
shit? Huh? Do you? Do you know I was standing in the
room when they were discussing finding my fucking sister
and torturing and killing her over some dumb shit like
this? I had to fear for my own life too because I had
walked in there cold, not knowing what the fuck to expect
because you wouldn't answer your phone. I didn't even
know if you were fucking dead or alive! Do you know
what I had to see? Do you have any fucking idea what I
witnessed behind your shit?" he barked at me. All of the
veins in his neck and face seemed to be pulsing. I had only
seen my brother this mad a few times before.

I stared at him, blinking rapidly as I waited for him to keep telling me how fucked-up of a person I was for saving a little girl from torture and further abuse.

"Oh, now you have a dumb look on your face, right? Well, apparently, you made a friend while you were in the club, right? Well, your little friend—just from whatever you said or did with him—someone obviously fucking noticed," Kyle gritted.

"A friend?" I contemplated for a few seconds. Then it seemed to hit me like a lightning strike. "Oh, Dee?" I asked, barely above a whisper. My body got cold and I started to shiver.

Kyle chuckled, but not in the way that said he thought something was funny. That chuckle was a true contradiction to the angry grimace on his face. He shook his head afterward, as if to say, *Really?*

"Yes, fucking Dee! Just from him talking to you, he got pulled into this bullshit. So while you were saving yourself and this little girl, let me show you what I walked in on happening to him. Just for fucking saying something to you, they thought he was down with your little escape plan. You want to see what you caused?" Kyle growled, jutting his cell phone toward my face so I could view the secret video he'd recorded. I sucked in my breath and my eyes widened as I watched . . .

"Help me! Oh, God, help me!" Dee had bawled, the veins in his face and neck had corded at the surface of his skin. Blood had mixed with his tears and made a mess all over his face, neck, and chest. His legs trembled and his teeth chattered.

"Oh, Derek . . . Derek . . . Derek, not even God can help you right now, my friend," Detective Keith had chortled as he circled Dee like a buzzard over a carcass. "Only you can help yourself right now Derek. *Only you.*"

"Ah, I told you everything I know," Dee had cried, his chin falling to his chest. He was exhausted. It had been hours since he'd been snatched from his post at the hotel. It had been five and half hours that he'd endured Detective Keith's torture.

"I'ma ask you one more time. Who is the girl you brought to the hotel? Where did she come from, and why did you let her in?" Detective Keith growled, his gun glinting at Dee every time he moved. Everyone in the room knew that Detective Keith had been Barker's number one enforcer for years, and he had a 100 percent confession rate.

"I . . . I swear . . . I don't—" Dee had cried, but never got to finish. "Agh!" he howled. His words tumbled back down his throat like hard marbles as one of Keith's goons cut a deep gash into the skin and muscles of his right thigh.

"C'mon, I hate to do this to you, but I need the answer. Who is the girl? We fucking saw you give her a key! You gave her a key to the boss's room!" Detective Keith had barked.

Dee shook his head left to right. "No . . . no . . . I . . ." He was gasping. "Agh!" he squealed again, bucking his body violently.

This time he screamed because Detective Keith twisted the knife in circles, digging farther into Dee's thigh muscle. Detective Keith had let out an exasperated breath and stood up. He stepped back a few paces and examined the mess of a man in front of him. He turned his head to the side and spit on the floor next to Dee.

"There is nothing worse in my eyes than a fucking weak traitor. Is she your woman? You fucking her?" he exploded.

Dee couldn't move or answer anymore. He looked to me like he was fading from shock.

"You playing tough, huh?" Detective Keith grumbled. "You must've brought her inside to fucking set us up. Is that what you did, Derek? Huh? Who paid you off? What did you gain from giving her that fucking room key? Who fucking paid you?!"

Again Dee didn't answer; he just had his head hanging like he was on his last leg of life.

Detective Keith had turned around and grabbed a box of iodized salt from the small metal table behind him. He smiled evilly. A collective gasp rose and fell around the room from the other workers forced to watch Detective Keith's maniacal behavior unfold right in front of them.

"Now, Derek, I'm a reasonable guy, wouldn't you say?" Detective Keith taunted. Dee didn't respond. "I want to help you, help yourself here. All you got to do is be smart about this. Be a good little boy and tell me if it was a setup. Did someone pay you off to bring that girl inside?" Detective Keith said evenly. But that quickly changed. "Tell me!" he exploded, causing Dee to jerk his head up and jump fiercely. Detective Keith circled Dee, shaking the box of salt menacingly. "That's what you did, isn't it? You brought her inside so you could let her set us up."

"No. I. Swear," Dee had panted out each word; it was a mixture of dribble and blood leaking from his lips. "Pl-pl-please. I swear, I . . . didn't," Dee had pleaded.

"Wow, I must give it to you, my man, you're just so fucking tough to crack. Your loyalty to whoever you're working with is more important than your own life, I guess!" Detective Keith barked. His eyes were hooded over with malice. With that, he emptied the entire box of salt into the open wounds covering Dee's body, taking time to crush some of the salt down into the huge gaping holes on Dee's thigh.

"Agh!" Dee squealed, his body bucking so fiercely against the chair and restraints that the chains binding him cut farther into his skin. More gasps filtered around the room, including from Kyle.

Unfazed, Detective Keith moved close to Dee's down-turned head so that he could whisper in his ear. "Whoever sent you is going to die. The only reason you live today is because I need you to find that girl and bring her to us. I want you both to die together, since you're working to-gether to be fucking traitors," Detective Keith hissed like a venomous snake.

Dee continued to hang his head. He looked like he was in so much pain, he wished for death.

"Take him out of my fucking sight," Detective Keith in-structed some of the guys standing around.

When the video was finished, I slid down to the floor and held my head. I tugged at my hair on both sides. I felt sick to my stomach, which caused me to dry heave a cou-ple of times. I felt awful about what happened to that guy, knowing that he was completely innocent of what they were accusing him of. With the key card I had taken ear-lier behind his back, I had also slipped out of the room and into Barker's without Dee actually knowing. It was so unfair that he'd suffered behind my actions. I felt awful.

"I didn't mean for all of this to happen, Kyle. I swear I didn't. Dee didn't do anything wrong. He is really inno-cent. All he did was be nice to me throughout the night. He was the one who told me Barker had requested me in VIP. He approached me—I didn't approach him. But I could tell he had liked me," I confessed.

"And that's not all, Khloé. That's not the end of all the casualties you left behind when you decided not to play along with the game until we could actually do something about it without getting killed. Oh no, that is not all the damage you've caused," Kyle said, sounding almost like he was getting satisfaction out of dropping these bombs on me to make me upset. I guess he wanted me to feel as upset as he was at that moment.

I moved my hands from my eyes and looked up at my brother as he stood over me, still brooding and still trying to drive home the point that I had royally fucked up.

"What do you mean, 'that is not all'?" I asked as softly as I could without sending Kyle into another furious rant. My soft baby-voice trick didn't work.

"Barker was there, that's what I fucking mean by 'that is not all'!" Kyle boomed, bending down into my face again. "Do you know how significant that is? Huh?" he asked, standing back up so he could circle around me. "Do you have any fucking foggy idea what that means?" he asked.

I shrugged a little bit, as if to say, *No, I don't, so tell me.* I looked at Kyle, feeling like a child caught red-handed being bad. I felt like any moment Kyle would be banishing me to my room or a corner.

"Barker is never fucking present when these things go down. He usually stays away and lets Redds handle his dirty work. But not this time. For some reason he wanted to be in the room. He needed to see and make sure that Dee got taken care of—just like he is going to want to see and make sure you and then I get taken care of," Kyle explained.

"I didn't see him on your video. How do you know he was there?" I replied.

"Oh, because I fucking know he was there. He didn't show up on the video because Barker stood behind a two-way mirror watching Redds inflict that torture on Dee. I heard from a source that was inside the room with him that Barker hadn't taken his eyes off of Dee the whole time. That's how bad they want to know who you are and where you are and how you infiltrated their shit so easily," Kyle said, starting his pacing again. "And where do all roads lead? Back to me, that's where."

I was quiet. My mind was racing like cars on the NASCAR track. Kyle looked at me seriously. But Kyle wouldn't stop. No matter what, he was determined to drive home his point about everything I'd done. I wanted to put my hands up over my ears and block him out, but I knew that would just stoke the flames of the fire raging inside my brother. So I kept on listening.

"What you don't understand is Anton Barker took mad pleasure in watching the pain and suffering in that man's eyes and hearing his screams. He would do anything to protect his own interest, even have a man killed, when he has no real proof he did anything to him. You dragged that man into the middle of something that had nothing to do with him. He is innocent and now he is fucked-up. You think they're going to stop there? Dee don't know shit about you, but they will keep on thinking so, until he is dead," Kyle continued, slamming his right fist into his left palm for emphasis.

"I'm sorry, Kyle. I was just t-trying t-to . . ."

"Trying to what? Get yourself killed for a fucking news story?" Kyle boomed again. He stopped moving and exhaled loudly. I could tell he was willing himself to calm down. He moved closer to me, and his face and tone were a bit calmer now.

"Listen to me. You know this shit is serious. I heard that another contact at the Norfolk Police Department gave Barker pictures from the hotel surveillance videos, and they already reviewed some of the tapes from the club that night. They have many more to look at, including the ones of the back and back doors. I heard Detective Keith watched the videos from the hotel and now he's waiting for the rest of the club videos. This is going to show me letting you into the club through the back. It's going to show you all throughout the club, walking around, if you took pictures. It's going to show that and everything. Your face will be plastered in their minds as someone to be hunted and captured," Kyle relayed, his jaw going stiff and his eyebrows dipping on his face.

I shook my head and started crying again. "I didn't mean for all of this to happen."

"There are security cameras everywhere. We are fucked. They have people working for them at every agency, business, hospital—you name it—in Norfolk. I'd be surprised if someone at the TV station isn't on their dirty payroll. That's what I was trying to explain to you. I told you from the gate we would have to be very careful," Kyle went on.

I sniffled back my tears and closed my eyes tightly. I was growing weary of his lecturing now. It was done already. I couldn't go back and change it. Now it was time for us to come up with a plan to get out of it. To blow the lid off Barker before he could catch us.

"Before I left, I heard them discussing you. They talked about your hair color and eye color, which are both memorable. You're going to have to cut and dye your hair and wear contacts," Kyle said.

"Okay," I agreed, getting up from the floor. "But I have to leave here and meet up with the girl Shara, the one that was in the room with Barker when I took the girl and escaped. I need the video she has before I go to the studio to get the story across to Christian. The faster I can get it, the better and faster we can get this over with," I said, rushing my words out in a huff.

"So you didn't hear a word I just said? You're in danger!" Kyle boomed again. "I don't know what the fuck kind of cement your head is made out of, but I'm not with the shits. You're not going to die on my watch and have Mama blaming me for the rest of my life. That is, if I even make it out of it alive myself," Kyle went on.

He stood brooding, his chest rising and falling rapidly. He turned toward me. "There is no way you can go meet up with anyone. You cannot trust that girl not to have you set up," he said evenly. "You will have to let that part of the story go."

"No, I need it. It's how we are going to save ourselves," I demanded.

"I told you everything would've come out in due time. Now you're wanted and I am probably next . . . and all for what?" Kyle said with feeling. He put his hands on his head and paced some more.

The little girl walked over; her eyes were filled with tears. "I can leave. I can make it better if I just go," she whimpered. "I don't want you to be in trouble."

I rushed over to her. "No, you're staying here until I can figure something out," I told her. Despite what my brother was talking about, this was a baby. There were many more to save on top of that. I wasn't giving up, no matter how angry Kyle got.

"You're going to keep going and going until all the casualties are too many to count," Kyle grumbled.

"I promise, this one last thing is all I need to do and then I will break the story, and this will all be behind us. You have to trust me," I said.

"Trusting you is how we got here. Now, where the fuck do you have to go to get this video?" Kyle asked, finally relenting.

I didn't dare smile outwardly, but I was smiling inside. Soon I was going to have the satisfaction of knowing I'd brought down the biggest fucking crime syndicate in the entire state of Virginia. A day that would make history— and my name would be all over it.

11

EVIDENCE COLLECTION

Ilooked at myself one more time in the long Victorian mirror standing in the corner of my bedroom. "I can't believe I had to cut my hair. And this color? Yuck. Definitely doesn't go with my eye color," I grumbled as I posed before the mirror, going over all of the changes I'd made to my appearance at the suggestion of my very worried twin brother. I sighed and picked up the dark shades I'd purchased too. I slid them on my face and looked one more time. To me, I didn't look like the same girl that had gone into the club that night, but who knows how I might look to the killers that were after me?

"These people got you out here looking crazy as hell, all in the name of a damn story. Risking life and limb—this is crazy," I scolded myself, then smiled. I was going to blow this story out of the water. So many heads were going to roll, it wasn't going to be funny. I had declared right there on the spot that I was going to win an Emmy for my reporting on Anton Barker and his crimes. I had said, manifested it, and claimed it.

I turned around and examined myself from the back to make sure the hidden microphone I had put on wasn't showing or too bulky. Kyle was going to be pleased that I had taken so many precautions before my meeting. I thought I could get used to this covert reporting stuff, but every time I did it, I think I lost another five years on my life. I'd barely been sleeping or eating or living, for that matter. All in the name of getting this story. It was crazy. The pressure, the danger, and the thrill of it all made me crazy.

I rushed out of the bathroom and stood in front of Kyle. "How do I look? You think anyone will recognize me as the old me?"

He grunted and his eyes said I looked good and different, but he wasn't happy about it at all. It had taken a whole lot of convincing to get him to agree to my meeting with Shara.

"You look different, but the same, if that makes sense," Kyle grumbled, looking me up and down. "This is mad risky, twin. You really have to be careful. You don't know that girl and you especially don't know if this is all a setup to get you," he warned. He answered me in the ominous voice he'd been speaking in for the last three days, since he'd come to my apartment wilding out. Kyle still wasn't convinced this was a good idea, but I didn't see any other way. I needed to collect the evidence for my story.

"I'll be fine," I assured him. I looked over at the little girl and made sure she understood that no matter what happened, she could not—absolutely could not—leave the apartment, use the phone, answer the door . . . nothing. I told her if anyone came here, she was to hide and not come out. If I didn't return in more than three days, then she needed to call the police.

"You never told me your name. What is it?"

"Maria."

"Okay, Maria, do you understand everything I am saying? This is a matter of life or death—everyone's life, including yours. Do you understand me?" I asked, shaking her shoulders to emphasize the importance of what I was telling her. She nodded her head. She didn't seem as upset about being alone as I had expected. On the other hand, my nerves had all of the hairs on my body standing at attention. As I left my apartment and headed to Kyle's car, I pep talked myself all the way there: *You got this. You got this. You're going to be a hero and a star. You will make it out alive and all will be well.* That was all I had to go off of—my own positive thoughts.

"I want you to make sure I can see you from out here at all times, which means find a spot near a window or something," Kyle said as the car approached the meeting spot. His breathing got heavier and I could see him gripping the steering wheel for dear life. His reaction to being there made my heartbeat speed up too. I was nervous, but for some reason I wasn't falling-apart nervous like Kyle was. Maybe he was right. Maybe I wasn't taking this thing as seriously as I should. I shrugged in my mind but wouldn't dare shrug my shoulders for my brother to see. That would've really set him off.

"I'll do my best. I have to go off of what Shara is comfortable with. Remember, when I spoke to her, she was adamant about me coming alone. If she sees you lurking, she may run away, and then we took this risk for nothing," I told Kyle.

He slammed his fist against the steering wheel. "I'm not going to tell you again! She could be setting you up! You are the one that needs to dictate everything for this meeting! Not her!" Kyle yelled. "Don't be fucking hardheaded all of your life!"

I put my hand up. "Okay, okay. No need to go crazy

again. I know this has been rough, but after today I'm going to break this story and it'll all be behind us, Kyle," I assured, keeping my voice low so I didn't upset him any more than he already was.

"All I'm saying, be smart and be safe, twin. I can't control what happens if I'm not there. The last time I left you alone, shit went haywire and you became a wanted woman in Norfolk," Kyle said.

"I get it. I'm going to be careful and smart, just like you taught me," I replied. "When this is all said and done, you're going to be so proud of your sister. You may be two minutes older than me, but I'm going to be the example. You watch me work," I said, nudging him on the arm with the hope that a little bit of light joking would take the edge off for both of us.

"Whatever, man. Just get in and get out," he replied. "No small talk. Get what you need from that bitch and get back out here. Simple. Don't be your usual extra-ass self. No time for the histrionics and extra drama today."

"Well, damn, I love you too. With your grumpy ass," I joked as I grabbed my oversized purse and prepared to get out of the car.

Kyle looked at his watch and then over at me. "You got thirty minutes to get in and out. If you ain't back here in thirty, I'm going to assume you got set up and I'm coming up in there, guns blazing. So watch the time and don't go even one minute over the thirty minutes, or else all hell is going to break loose," Kyle said, his tone serious and his face stony.

I wore a goofy smile, trying to lighten Kyle's mood and, at the same time, curb my own nerves. All I could do, now that I was at the meeting place, was pray that Shara had kept her word and she hadn't been coaxed into setting me up for the kill.

* * *

I exited the car and rushed toward the restaurant, head down, eyes and head covered. I felt the little gun Kyle had given me digging into my side as I moved quickly. When I made it to the front door of the small café, I looked around, checked my immediate surroundings, and then entered. Once inside, I was relieved that the place only had a few patrons who all seemed like the retirement types—older folks reading newspapers or thick, dog-eared paperback novels while sipping coffee.

Just like I'd been asked to do, and against everything Kyle had instructed me to do, I went straight to the back of the quaint little eatery. A flash of excitement hit me when I spotted Shara and she was indeed alone. I stood up a bit taller and walked a bit faster. I was so excited, tears welled up in my eyes right away. They'd come out of nowhere. I guess I was relieved that she was okay after I'd left her in that hotel suite with sick-ass Anton Barker. It was the first emotion I had allowed myself to feel other than terror for the past three days. I squeezed both of my hands so tightly, my nails dug into my palms.

Shara looked down at her watch. She picked up her glass of red wine and took a sip. Finally she spotted me. She sat up a little straighter. Shara watched as I tried my best to smoothly and calmly walk toward her. Still, she jumped as I slid into the booth opposite her. She and I both let out long breaths. She greeted me with a tiny smile and nod, which kind of eased my anxiety.

"Why so jumpy?" I asked.

"You never know who is watching," she said nervously. "I'm sure you feel just as on edge as I do."

I nodded. I definitely did.

Shara looked like she was starting to calm down faster than I expected so that put me a little more at ease as well.

Had Shara been looking around like she was expecting someone, I would've been on alert that this whole thing might be a setup. She also looked much better than she had the night I saw her in the club and in that hotel suite with Barker. Gone were the half-fitting blond lace-front wig, too-tight dress, and the gaudy makeup. Today she wore a bare face; the discoloration around her eye was almost gone. The Adidas tracksuit, and her hair hung curly in its natural state was really nice. She was beautiful from up under all that shit she had on that night at the club. I was amazed at how much younger she looked now.

"Well? Do you have everything I asked for?" I got right to the point.

"Yeah," she said, placing a manila envelope on the table. I reached out for it, but Shara put her hand over mine and stopped me.

"Oh. Oh, yes. I . . . I . . . didn't forget," I stammered. I reached down next to me, dug into my purse, and retrieved a thick, overstuffed, letter-sized white envelope. I extended my hand under the table toward Shara. She reached under the table and took the envelope from me.

"You can be sure it is all there. Trust me," I said. "I know you went through a lot to do what you're doing, and I'm going through a lot to do what I'm doing as well."

Shara gave the envelope a squeeze.

"Feels about right," she said. Then she released the envelope to me.

"There are a few things you need to know," she said, leaning in closer to the table.

I stared at Shara intently. "Go ahead. I'm listening."

"They are really scouring the streets for the little girl that you took. They're not going to rest until they find her . . . and you. I heard the boss, the one we were with that night, say that he wanted to personally kill you himself for what you did. They will not stop until they find you—even if it's years from now," Shara relayed.

I felt my chest tighten. I picked up the glass of water in front of me, my hands trembling.

"You all right?" Shara asked.

I nodded my head. "I'm fine," I lied.

"There are pictures and a video of the other little girls in the package that were taken from the pin camera. Apparently, there are a bunch of those same-aged girls being housed somewhere. They farm them out when they need to, for the sick pleasure of some very high-up politicians. Oddly enough, Barker never usually deals with the little ones . . . only us big ones. But that night it was like he was on something. Strange," Shara continued.

"What about his recent activities?" I pressed, flattening my hands on the envelope.

Shara shifted uncomfortably in her seat. "That I'll let you see for yourself," she said, bringing her nails up to her mouth to bite them nervously. "It's not the kind of thing I'd talk about in public."

I swallowed hard. "That bad, huh?"

"You'll have to judge for yourself. I just did what you asked of me," Shara said. "Now, just like I told you, I'm taking this money and getting as far away from here as I possibly can. I'll never be able to go back around him or them or anywhere in the area and be safe, once you expose all of this. He will know right away who gave you the videos and pictures. So, good luck," she said.

I picked up the envelope and held it against my chest. I didn't know what exactly I'd find inside, but something Shara had said had struck a chord with me.

"Oh, and one more thing," Shara said, looking at me like she felt sorry for me. "I need to give you more real important information that I got."

I raised my eyebrows and also leaned closer to the table. My facial expression asked all of the questions without her having to utter a word.

"So the lady that helped you escape from the hotel, in the car?" Shara started. She paused and looked out into the café, as if someone else could hear her. "Word on the street is they found her after looking at the hotel cameras. They got her license plate and had someone in the police department run her plate and find her address," Shara whispered, her eyes widening.

I sucked in my breath and didn't realize I had my hand cupped over my mouth.

"It gets worse," Shara continued, leaning farther into the table.

I stared at her blankly for a few minutes. My heart began hammering against my chest bone. The thoughts running through my head already had my blood pressure rising.

"I heard them talking about going to her house. A source close to the inside said they had beat and tortured her, because they wanted her to tell them where you were and how she knew you. They said she couldn't tell them anything because she didn't remember. They weren't buying it though. So now I heard that they're throwing your description around in the streets. Niggas is looking for a chick with hazel eyes, sandy brown hair, light skin, and your whole physical size." Shara paused and lowered her voice. "He is not going to stop until he has you in his grasps, even if it is years from now. He vowed to kill you and I heard it with my own ears," she whispered. Her words resounded like bombs exploding in my ears.

I sat back from the table and let out a long sigh. I didn't know how to respond to the information.

"Sounds like he's going through a lot just to hide his tracks. There are a million chicks with hazel eyes and sandy brown hair in the world," I replied, trying to play it off like I wasn't literally falling apart inside.

Shara looked at me as if to say, *Is this bitch getting the seriousness of what I am saying?*

"I'm telling you, he is ruthless. They are saying this dude Barker doesn't give up. He has his people move in silence and violence. You won't even see him and his people coming, because most people don't even expect him to be a part of this underworld life. He only has a trusted few that get to be in his presence, even though they saying he got clients with at least seven hundred distributors on the East Coast between New York and Miami working for him. I think you should get out of town for good, like me," Shara said softly. "For real. This is too close for comfort. It doesn't take shit for his dirty DTs or somebody to eventually find you. They are definitely working hard at it right now. Get out," she finished ominously.

I shook my head left to right before the words even fully left Shara's mouth. "Nah. I ain't leaving town. I'm not scared of no fucking crooked, drug-dealing politician. I have a few more people to see and then I have a story to tell. So right now, I'm here to stay until I see this all the way through until the end," I said stubbornly.

"I hope your stubbornness doesn't cost you your life. Look, I never got a chance to say it, but thank you for saving that little girl. It cost me a black eye and some gut punches, but I'm still here and standing," Shara whispered as she pointed to the discoloration in the corner of her eye. "This ain't about just me or you, or even her. It's about all of it. All of those innocent babies. If you can save them, please do it."

"Not if I run out of town like a coward. That bastard will pay for everything he is doing, once I expose his ass. I want to see that bitch-ass nigga, eye to eye, on the courthouse steps, when he is indicted and convicted of every single crime he has committed. I will stare him down and he will know then who was responsible for taking his black ass down," I said, feeling powerful on the inside.

"I'm really sorry you have to do all this shit alone. Once you stepped into it like you have, I guess you have no choice but to see it through. But after you take care of it all, you need to go off the grid for a while. I'm telling you, this dude Barker has you in his eye for revenge. I don't think it will even matter if you take him down. His reach goes so far, he might have people after you for the rest of your life. And once that evidence comes out, it won't be long before he puts it together that it was me who gave you everything you needed," Shara said.

I shook my head. "I thank you for looking out, but don't worry about me. I'm a big girl and I can handle anything that comes my way," I told Shara confidently. "If he is so powerful and so omniscient, like some sort of a god, then he can get out there and come find me. I can't wait to meet him."

Shara looked at me and shook her head. She looked like she'd finally figured out that with me there was no winning. I was going forward with my story, no matter how big, mean, and scary Anton Barker's threats got.

"Well, I don't think I'm untouchable, like you seem to think you are. My grandma always told me that all of the baddest motherfuckers are already six feet under. Remember I told you that," Shara said pointedly.

I smirked. "But she forgot that some of those bad motherfuckers are in prison and have been put there by thorough reporters like me," I came back. "Now, changing the subject. You take care of yourself and stay away from men like Anton Barker," I said, my voice taking on a friendlier tone.

"I will. I ain't wasting no time. First thing I'm going to

do is go shopping. Shit, I ain't had this much cash at one time in a long minute," Shara joked, lightening the mood.

"Have at it," I joked back. "Let's order something, I haven't eaten in three days," I confessed.

Shara and I sat there like old pals who had just come to meet for lunch, but I could tell that both of our minds were racing in different directions at that moment. Still, we were going to make the best of being together again for what was more than likely the last time.

12

BREAKING NEWS

"Where are all of the segment write-ups? Who has my questions for the mayoral candidate debate? Did anyone do current background on Belle Switson? I hear that after all of her arrests and money troubles, she is now running for mayor as well. Is that true? Has anyone endorsed her? How long is Amber's new segment that will air before my moderation of the debate? Does anyone have an idea on where Khloé is and what her exclusive is about?"

I rushed into the station to find Christian blasting questions and demands at the team as she sat in the hair and makeup chair, preparing for the big Norfolk mayoral candidate debate. The staff was running around in circles trying to be responsive to all of her requests. Her assistant, Darla, handed her a stack of papers to read in the meantime.

"So wait a minute. No one has heard from Khloé? Is this girl playing with me? She told me she has something so big that I would want to see her before we air the debate, and she's not even here?" Christian went on, glancing over the document in front of her. Darla nodded her head, affirming.

"Damn shame," Christian said, shaking her head. "I keep giving these dumbass junior reporters chance after chance and they just don't get it. Ugh!" she growled, throwing the papers up in the air until they rained down around her.

"You have to keep still or your face is going to look like Miss Piggy on crack," Christian's makeup guy demanded. Her hairstylist groaned, nodding her head in agreement.

"I'm sorry. I know I am being a complete pain in the ass right now. I just need everything to be right for this debate segment. There are so many things I need to get done before we start the live airing." Christian kind of apologized, realizing she was being a bitch on wheels. Everyone knew Christian's nerves were on edge because the station chief was hounding her about the recent drop in WXOT-TV's ratings.

After taking a little time off of work at the last minute to get her personal life together, Christian's work had suffered. Amber was left in charge while she was gone, and perhaps that was the biggest mistake Christian had made. If she knew better, Christian would be able to see that her little protégée was trying to sabotage her career. I don't know why Christian thought Amber was more capable than anyone else of holding things down while she was gone; but now, from the sound of things, she knew she'd been wrong.

"I still want to know what happened to this big exclusive Khloé said she was working on? She probably made that up to buy herself more time at the station. These girls can be so unreliable these days," Christian said again.

"Where is Amber? I need to know what she has on tap for tonight. It has to be good, but not so good that it overshadows me on TV with all of the mayoral candidates," Christian called out. "Goddamn, why is everyone here but Khloé?"

I finally stepped out of the shadows to let her know I was indeed there. I knew she was hopeful that the mayoral debate would pull in enough ratings to save everyone's jobs, but I was going to have to tell her my plan to break my story, which would, of course, derail the entire airing of the mayoral debate. I was still trying to figure out how I was going to propose we call out Anton Barker on national television, all while trying to stay alive, knowing that he also had the police and a slew of other Norfolk government officials on his payroll.

"Christian . . . um . . . I—"

"Where have you been? What are you supposed to be presenting for tonight's segments?" Christian snapped, without even a greeting.

"There's something I wanted to tell you, but we need to speak in private," I said, wringing my hands together. This news wasn't something I could afford to blab out in front of everyone in the bustling station studio.

"I don't have time for this right now, Khloé. I need to know what you're going to do, and if whatever you have to say doesn't pertain to a ratings hit-level story, then get away from me and go speak to Amber or Darla about whatever problem or issue you have. I have entirely too much going on to deal with another thing right now," Christian said in agitation.

"But it's really important, and you might need to know this before—"

"Christian, the first mayoral candidate just arrived. And

the guest-receiving office says that another person, who is not on the list, is asking to see you as well. We have already checked Mr. Anton Barker into greenroom A. Your other visitor wasn't on the list, so you'll have to go escort them in," one of the station assistants called out, completely interrupting her and halting the conversation with me.

My shoulders tensed when I heard his name and I immediately wondered who was with him. "I tried to warn you," I mumbled as I watched Christian completely dismiss me without further acknowledgment.

"He is here, people. Anton Barker, the number one candidate on the list, is in the building. I need those questions. I will go over them before the debate. Let me go make sure he's comfortable. I want this all to go as smoothly as possible. And, not to mention, has anyone seen that fine specimen of a man," Christian yelled out, jumping down from her chair and walking while her hairstylist followed her with a can of hair spray, misting the air above her head.

"Where the hell is Amber? I still need information about her piece. Isn't this the second or third damn time I've asked for her? What the hell is she hiding from me?" Christian huffed, flustered. She threw her hands up and rushed off to greet the mayoral candidates as they started checking in.

I followed as Christian hurried down the long corridor that led to the studio's greenrooms. I stopped and watched as she pushed in the first door and found Barker standing inside, with his back turned, looking at the awards on the walls. Once Christian walked into the room, I rushed to the wall outside so I could listen.

"Mr. Barker!" Christian called excitedly. Barker whirled

around with a huge smile plastered on his face. They shared a quick, tight embrace. Christian stepped out of Barker's arms and took a good look at him.

"You are still as handsome as ever. I guess they can't keep a good man down, huh?" Christian commented, clearly flirting with Barker.

I gagged listening to her pander to him—if she only knew what was about to come out about her favorite.

"Nope. I know people probably expected me to be looking sad, distraught, and raggedy, but not all candidates take on that look after having their names falsely dragged through the mud. This was one mudslinging campaign," Barker answered. "You're looking good yourself. Nice and young," he lied.

"Thanks. Mr. Barker, if you only knew what I've been going through to get the exclusive rights to air and moderate this mayoral debate. This is the one chance you get to show off so that the whole city knows you are definitely the best qualified candidate up against a bunch of crackpots. I don't want anything to go wrong. I have been busting balls around here, trust me," Christian said. "Everyone is eager to hear you speak, especially since the media has given you such a bad rap for your past list of clients. Tuh, if anyone understands what it's like to claw your way up to the top, it is me."

Listening to Christian just go on and on about how great she thought Barker was immediately made me sick to my stomach. It also made me eager to drop the bombs I was hiding.

"Great. Truth be told, I have only done what every other candidate would've done—follow the letter of the law," Barker replied, lying like the crooked bastard that he was.

"I know that's right. But in other news, it has been ages since we've seen each other, and it's been on my mind to call you up. We haven't had time to go to our usual lunches, dinners, hangouts, nothing. We need to get together and catch up. I've got lots of new and interesting things to share," Christian said with a hint of mystery in her voice.

I almost fainted! She was friends or lovers, or something, with Barker in the past? What? It was a good damn thing I hadn't revealed my story to her too early. She would've definitely put the kibosh on it. I couldn't believe what I was hearing. My head started swimming and I felt slightly dizzy.

"I miss you and the time we spent together, Christian. There has just been so much going on with both of us. We really have to do better. Once I am mayor, I promise we will pick back up," Barker insisted.

I wanted desperately to jump out and scream at both of them that Barker was a fucking lying, perverted, child-fucking criminal, but I decided I would leave it all for my planned blowup of the story. If I wasn't leery of Christian's loyalty before, I damn sure knew I needed to be now. At the end of the day, I was a news reporter first, but it seemed Christian had a lot of personal connections that she let get in the way. I knew I had to be careful with the information I was about to disclose now. I was completely blown to find out that Christian had a relationship with Barker all along. It definitely made me think of her differently now.

"So, are you really ready for this?" Christian asked.

Barker inhaled deeply and let out a long breath. He looked at Christian seriously.

"Honestly, Christian, I don't think I've ever been more ready for something in my life. It's time for me to set the record straight on a few things and to claim this seat. The media and the public have the wrong idea about me and about everything that went down. I just really want people to know that I am not a monster that set out to keep criminals out on the street. People act like I woke up one day and said, 'Today I'm going to defend criminals and rub elbows with them.' So far from the truth. I was paid for a service. I love the letter of the law. I had to do my job, and criminal defense is my job. I stood up in those courtrooms and did my job to the best of my ability. I can't be expected to just roll over and play dead because of the public perception of me for who I represent.

"Was I paid a good bit of money for my services? Well, yes. But that is what I went to school for. Being a damn good criminal defense attorney is my lifeblood. I prided myself on it, and no matter who my clients were, I wanted to do a good job. Just like what I want to do as mayor of Norfolk. That is a topic I will definitely address tonight. I want to tell my story for all of the citizens out there listening. Can you believe that people are actually following me and wanting to vote for me? And that is why I would never fold to the pressure. There are people who want to see me win in this city, but there are also people that, for whatever reason, want to see me fail," Barker explicated, shaking his head in disgust.

I was sick. I swayed on my weak legs and my stomach swirled. What a fucking lying bastard he was. I must admit, Barker had the gift of gab. I could see why so many people followed him and planned to vote for him. I had heard enough. I had to go get ready for what was about to go down.

As I went to rush away from the door, I ran into Liza. She looked disheveled and upset.

"Sorry," she said after she bumped into me.

"Are you all right?" I asked her.

"You know, I'm not. I'm so tired of the treatment around her. Christian has been a complete bitch for weeks, and then she left that bitch Amber in charge, and you know what I just found out?" Liza ranted, her face turning completely red.

"What? What did you find out?" I asked, aghast that Liza was even speaking that much. I had never heard her talk that much since I'd been at WXOT-TV.

"I found out Amber stole my story line for tonight. Tonight—one of the biggest-ratings nights we will ever have, and she's stolen my story. I am looking for her, and when I find her, all hell will break loose. I'm sick of her and Christian and everyone!" Liza said with feeling.

"I completely understand where you're coming from" I said, playing into the gossip. Liza was genuinely shocked by the revelation. "I'm so sorry you had to go through all of that. I'm so disappointed in Christian. But it's the nice girls like us that sometimes get the raw end of the deal. But don't worry, trust me when I say, every dog has its day," I said sagaciously.

After we talked, Liza and I stood aside and let the others do their thing. I recruited her to help me set up what I had planned. I felt like she would get just as much satisfaction out of blowing up shit at the news station as I was going to get. When I finally decided to blow the story out of the water, I no longer cared about whether or not Christian gave me that 6:00 p.m. news job. My motivation was totally different now. Luring Anton Barker to the station was the best thing Christian could've ever done for me. She just didn't know it yet. She had actually made my job much easier now. God was also on my side, because had Barker not come to the new station for the debate, I would've never been able to blow him up like I was about to do now.

"Unfortunately, after I blow this story, I might have to leave the city that I love and where I've been all of my life. I will have to leave my mother behind, for sure, and may even have to go into hiding for years and years," I explained to Liza as we set up for the big blowup. It was so sad that men like Barker were affecting people's lives so much—even mine—and I was just the reporter that was going to blow the lid off his ass.

"I'm so glad to have women like you in my corner to get through things together. Khloé, I am so glad we spoke today. Trust me, it may not always seem like I am smart, but I realize that I don't care about this job anymore either. This news station has taken my soul," Liza said.

"I feel the same way. I'm always selling my soul for this place, and what have I ever gotten in return? *Nothing*. Nothing but criticism and heartache," I agreed with her.

Liza and I had been made to question everyone's intentions and loyalty at the station. But our revelations to each other indicated a level of trust and confidence that I previously doubted would ever exist at that job. Maybe a true friendship could be forged amongst the junior reporters that Christian treated like trash, after all.

"How does my makeup look?" I asked Liza. "Can't be blowing up people on TV looking like a dry-face hen. I also can't have raccoon eyes for this very important shot."

Liza chuckled. "You look perfect. This is all going to be perfect and I can't wait to see their faces."

"C'mon, follow me. You are my special assistant now, so you don't have to sit in here and wait. You can come on air with me. It'll probably be both of our first and last time on air here at WXOT. But, whatever, we have to do it," I said, heading for the door. Liza followed me out into the hallway.

"I love that outfit, by the way," Liza complimented. Her spirit seemed renewed after unloading the burdens of her work life.

"Thanks. Can't ever go wrong with a sophisticated blouse and pencil skirt. I was a little worried. I thought I was going to have to hear that bitch Christian yell at me for wearing this color or that color or this shoe or that shoe," I said, mocking Christian with my hand movements.

"You have no idea how she would've carried on. 'Yellow? Oh, my God, what are you? A fucking banana,'" Liza replied, also mocking Christian. We chuckled. As we stepped into the hallway, we saw Christian and Barker rushing down the walkway. I pulled Liza into an empty corner, so they didn't see us.

"Ms. Aniston, you have another guest," a staff member reminded Christian.

"Oh, really? Who could this be now? All of the candidates should already be in their rooms and ready to take the stage in a few minutes," Christian said, seemingly embarrassed in front of Barker.

"It's fine. You have a job to do, I'm not the most important guest here," he said, smirking. "I think we are finished with our missing-you moment anyway. It's probably one of the other candidates, but I don't know why they're going to bother checking in. You wait until I get to that debate stage, there will be no man left standing. I bet they will all be pulling out of the race and scrambling when I'm done," Barker promised.

Liza and I raced down the stairs so we could get a firsthand view of who was coming to the station now. When Christian and Barker stepped off of the elevator into the lobby and headed toward the guest reception desk, we all saw her so-called guest. The smile on Christian's face quickly folded into a scowl. She had been yapping away, but her words went tumbling back down her throat as soon as she laid eyes on her visitor. I'm sure she didn't waste any time coming up with an immediate conspiracy theory in her head.

"Did you plan this?" Barker gritted, confronting Christian with his eyes ablaze in anger. "Did you set me up?"

"No, I wouldn't do that. I had no idea," Christian answered, almost breathlessly. She was just as shocked and dumbfounded as Barker.

Barker folded his arms across his chest defiantly. Christian didn't exactly have a pristine reputation for telling the truth.

"Sure seems like a setup to me," he pressed on.

"Trust me, Anton, I wouldn't spring something like this on you. I . . . I . . . don't know anything about this," Christian assured.

Liza and I watched, elated. "It worked," Liza whispered to me.

"It sure did," I confirmed, smiling.

Suddenly all of the little girls and the entire group of people erupted into their protest chants.

"Barker is a criminal! We don't want him in our government!"

"Arrest Anton Barker! Arrest Anton Barker!"

"Anton Barker is a child predator! Anton Barker deserves the death penalty! Down with Anton Barker!"

I felt so excited and vindicated at the same time. That

was part of my handiwork coming to fruition. I just wished Kyle was there to see this part. I'm sure he would see what else I had in store for Anton Barker's ass.

"I suggest you handle this or else my participation in this debate will be called off. I don't like this kind of sneaky shit, Christian," Barker said, his jaw stiff as a board. His people were looming around him, ready to pounce at any moment.

I could tell Christian's blood was boiling. She would say she didn't need this kind of drama before she went on television.

"Wait right here. I will take care of this forthwith. Trust me, I had no idea something like this would be happening, because you know I wouldn't tolerate this shit. You just wait right here and let me take care of it," Christian told Barker. She stormed past the reception desk to the group of protestors.

I was so proud to see all of those little girls lined up in the front like a united front. My brother had risked his life for those little girls. I just knew Barker wanted to die inside after seeing every single one of those little faces that he could surmise would one day be staring at him in a court of law.

"What the hell are you doing here?" Christian asked, wasting no time with small talk. "You can't just pop up at my station like this—no warning, nothing. You are disturbing the peace and I will have all of you arrested! I don't care about children either!"

"We are here to tell you that Anton Barker is a child predator, sex trafficker, and criminal," one girl said, stepping forward into Christian's face.

"Get out of here! You will not ruin this ratings sweep for me!" Christian barked, trying to break free of the security guards who were creating a barrier between her and the protestors.

"Let go of me! I'm not playing. So help me, God, I will walk all of you into the goddamn jailhouse myself. I don't care how young any of you are, you will not ruin tonight's debate with all of your nasty and vile allegations and lies," Christian spat.

"We will have our voices heard, no matter what you say," one of the protestors spoke up.

"You don't have the right or a permit to gather here. Now, if you don't leave, I will have the police, the dogs, the hoses, or whatever it takes to get you people out of my station," Christian said forcefully. "We don't indulge all of this fake-civil-rights shit on my watch."

Liza and I locked eyes for a brittle few seconds. I felt my heart breaking into a million pieces when I listened to Christian's racist comments. That bitch had some nerve, and I was about to show her just who was going to have the police take them out of the station.

"Let's go upstairs to the floor," I told Liza.

"This is going to be crazy. I hope you're ready for all of the backlash that is going to come," Liza said, as if she was already having second thoughts.

"I don't care. What no one understands is this is about right and wrong, not a silly story anymore. This is not something I can just act like I don't know. That man slept with children, killed people, stole from people, and did all sorts of dirty deeds," I explained as we walked.

"I am going to be cheering you on from the sidelines and I am ready to make that call as soon as you give me the signal. This will explode into chaos here in the studio, but I am ready to stick by your side. Anything to see Christian's entire career fall apart before my eyes," Liza said, giving my arm a reassuring squeeze.

"And don't worry, no matter what, I will make sure you get credit for everything you've helped me with today, assisting with setting up this story to be aired," I promised.

"Good luck," Liza said.

"Thanks, I'm going to need all the luck I can get," I said.

13

PLAYING THE WAITING GAME

I walked past the room where Barker was waiting and pacing. "I'm so sorry again. I had no idea anything like this was going to happen. I wanted to give you a leg up in the race. That was the reason I fought so hard for the debate to air here," Christian appealed.

Barker's eyebrows shot up in surprise. "So it was a *favor*? *I* am doing a favor, not the other way around, so let's just make that clear. In fact, I think I will just leave," he replied.

Christian looked like she would faint when he said that. She rushed in front of him with her hands clasped together like she was praying. "Anton, I am sorry. From the bottom of my heart, I am sorry. I can't say that enough. I am sorry this ended up happening. But I need you to do this debate. My ass is on the line. All of the advertisers that paid for tonight will have my head and my job on the chopping block," Christian pleaded.

"Really? That's what you're going with? You're worried about advertisers when there are people out there shouting that I am a pervert and child sex trafficker," Barker shot back, hardening his stance.

"No, I am not just worried about advertisers. I have been your friend forever and I want to see you win. I want to see you take this city and turn it around. I believe you're the man who can do that. I believe that if you become mayor, I can be the best press secretary you've ever seen," Christian said, confessing her real intentions.

A light knock on the a jarred door interrupted their little confessional. I turned on my heels and got ready. Liza had given me the thumbs-up that said she had everything in place. She was ready for her role as well.

"Who is it?" Christian barked.

"Liza" she answered in her famous meek voice.

"What is it?" Christian yelled peevishly. Liza pushed the door further back and stuck her head through the opening, just like we had rehearsed.

"I wanted to talk to you before the segments air on television. You might want to preview Amber's first," Liza said tentatively. I was impressed by how good she was at being a distraction.

"Okay, damn it. I've been looking for her ass all day." Christian sucked her teeth. She followed Liza down to the main stage and watched the edit screens in the back. I could see her from where I stood and I smirked at her.

Christian looked around. "What is she doing up there? What is going on? I haven't approved anything she is going to air. Where is Amber?" Christian shot questions rapid-fire now. I could not only hear her, but I could also see that she was uneasy.

"I'm sorry, Christian. We can continue our discussion later, but for now, I suggest you watch this first. I'm sure your ratings and your job are depending on this," Liza said curtly.

Everyone's eyes went to the screens and were on me at the same time. I appeared on the screen with a wide, blazingly white smile.

"Taught her well." Christian smiled proudly. As she listened to my news piece, her smile quickly faded.

"Tonight I bring you a WXOT-TV breaking-news exclusive. The rumors about criminal defense attorney, and now Norfolk mayoral candidate, Anton Barker engaging in several criminal enterprises are all true. These photographs obtained by WXOT show Barker and underage girls in various compromising positions. As you know, Barker and his wife share a son. He is not only a husband, but a father. Unfortunately, it looks like Barker is also an unconscionable pedophile who has had people killed to keep his secrets. Barker wasn't the only government official involved. There is much more evidence, and we will be bringing it all to you live throughout this broadcast."

I could see Christian moving her hands animatedly behind the scenes. I didn't care. I continued with my broadcast breaking news. When I was done, I stormed off the set and met Christian, toe to toe.

All of the color faded from Christian's face; her mouth hung open until her chin almost hit her chest. Everyone around us stared, aghast. Christian's eyes hooded over and her fists were clenched.

"You fucking bitch! You hungry-for-a-story, low-down, dirty bitch!" Anton Barker appeared out of nowhere, directing his wrath at Christian. "I can't believe you would do this to me! After everything we have been through together!" he boomed, looking like he wanted to rip Christian's eyes out.

"Barker, wait! I swear I didn't know. I had no fucking idea she was going to do this. I would never do something like this to you. You have to believe me!" Christian stood her ground.

"Prove it, Christian! I don't trust you." Barker gnashed his teeth in disgust.

"I will prove it. Wait until I get my hands on that little bitch!"

Christian stormed toward me. I stood my ground, digging my heels into the floor, just in case she got the crazy idea that she could hit me or something.

A crowd followed, hot on Christian's heels. They all wanted to see the scene unfold, but I knew that in no time it was going to get even worse.

"Where is she? Where the fuck is she?" Christian screamed. All of the staff fell silent. She whirled around and found me looking dead at her.

"You planned this all along, didn't you? You fucking planned to embarrass me and him and you never told me shit!" Christian accused, getting within inches of my face.

"I tried to tell you several times what my story was about, but your head was too far up Amber's and Barker's asses to listen," I said boldly. "I tried to warn you several times, in fact. I wanted to meet with you for days, and all you could talk about was Amber's news story—which, by the way, I made up because I knew you'd give it to her to steal. You're no reporter, Christian Aniston. You're a power-hungry bitch looking for attention," I shot back.

Christian sucked her teeth and grabbed my arm. She dragged me toward an empty dressing room, pushing me inside and slamming the door like a madwoman. When she turned toward me, she took a fighting stance, kicked off her high heels, and moved in for the kill.

Before she could say a word, Barker barreled into the room, ranting.

"You bitch! *She* is the one who did this? How dare you let her do this to me! All for a fucking story and ratings!" Barker accused, charging forward toward me and Christian.

"Security!" Christian shrieked just before Barker could get to us.

"You were supposed to be my friend! You've ruined my life!" Barker screamed, still coming for us.

Christian jumped in the middle. I pulled out the little gun that Kyle had given me when we'd first started stalking Barker to get this story. I leveled it at him.

"Don't fucking come any farther," I gritted, the gun out in front of me and aimed straight for his chest. Even his security couldn't react fast enough. None of them expected me to be packing.

"Wait! Don't!" Liza screamed, trying to stop me from making a mistake. "You'll go to jail. It's not worth it," she yelled.

Christian slapped Liza across the face, knocking her back, just before security personnel swarmed into the dressing room. I quickly hid my gun and raced over to Liza.

The guards spoke to Christian, while Liza and I were quickly escorted into the hallway.

Before Christian closed the door, she asked the guard to bring me back inside. She wanted to deal with this without all of the studio staff interfering. She was ready to rip me to shreds.

"You little sneak. You knew exactly what you were doing! You knew better than to show me that story because you knew there was no way I would let you spew these lies about Barker. You also knew I was working on this debate for months. There's a difference between being cutthroat and being heartless." Christian pointed her finger in my face accusingly.

"Don't be a fucking hypocrite, Christian," I said condescendingly, still holding my ground. "Wasn't it you that said sometimes you have to go out there and make your own exclusive? Seduce a few people. Stalk some people. Whatever it takes. You didn't specify that your so-called friends were off limits. I watched you do the same shit for a couple of years. Remember what you did to Lucy Coles? You're scandalous. You tried to ruin her career and didn't think twice about it. That's why I don't respect your ass!" I spat.

"You are fired! You no longer work here. Pack your shit and get the hell out!" she ordered.

"Can't handle a dose of your own medicine, Christian?" I laughed gratingly. I called to Liza because she had the rest of my evidence.

"I said, 'You're fired.' When I come back here in five minutes, you and all of your shit better be gone," Christian hissed, the heat of her breath burning on my lips.

"You can't get rid of me that easily, Christian," I shot back, lowering my head and spitting at Christian's feet. "I'm here to stay. Can't you see that you're nothing without me here?" I said, sounding more confident than I'd ever been in my life. "You are me, and I am you. You get rid of me, and you get rid of yourself," I said, letting her know that the tables had officially turned at WXOT-TV.

"Oh, you don't think I can get rid of you? I call the fucking shots around here, you little wannabe. If I say you go, then you go. This is my show. You better remember who looked out for you and hired you when these folks were making you get coffee and pick up their fucking dry cleaning, you little upstart bitch," Christian reminded me.

"Well, here is the thing. If you fire me, you won't have a job either. In fact, if you get rid of me, by the time I am done ruining and embarrassing you and this entire place, you won't even be able to show your face in Norfolk ever again, much less be executive producer here at WXOT-TV," I hissed. "You'll be blacklisted from the industry, period."

"Nothing you can do or say can ruin or embarrass me. I don't get shamed that easily, bitch. Plus, you're a *nobody*. My name rings bells. Can you say the same for yours? I don't think so. Everyone knows you as the girl who wants to be just like Christian Aniston," Christian shot back.

"Oh no," I scoffed. "I beg to differ. The person who wants to be just like you is Amber, and she's not around now, is she?" I said mockingly. "Oops, did I just say that? Yes, I did. Where was she when you needed her? Nowhere to be found!" I folded my arms and laughed maliciously. "After I show you this, I think you'll change your fucking tune," I said as I picked up a remote and hit a button for the screen inside the room.

Christian's lips thinned and her face flushed with anger. She squinted her eyes in disgust. She could see Anton Barker from the back, and for the first time seeing his huge tattoo clearly visible on the screen. Christian put both of her hands on her stomach and bent slightly more with each passing second. In the darkness on the screen, Christian could hear a tiny voice screaming and pleading and saying no. It was mainly the voice, which sounded like a small child's, combined with what Barker was saying, that looked like it almost made Christian's heart stop. She listened, stunned, then covered her mouth with her hand to keep herself from screaming or vomiting. I clicked off the screen, sick to my stomach too.

"Now you see why I had to do this? Anton Barker is not only a criminal who takes bribes, and has people killed, but, most importantly and most disgustingly, he is a child rapist. I will tell the whole world that he raped children. With that video, even in the darkness, and that soundtrack, he will have no defense. I don't care if Johnnie Cochran was resurrected; Barker will be found guilty. I will play this footage for the cops, the media, YouTube. It will be everywhere. Barker will go to prison, and if you continue to associate yourself with him, like you've already done, you will never be able to show your face in this town again."

I leaned back and casually crossed my arms. "The station will most certainly fire you, because your being associated with the big scandal—that you wanted so badly—will be a distraction. Sound familiar? Isn't that how you got Lucy fired? Created a scandal around her name? Yeah, someone finally beat you at your own game, Christian. Your little friends won't be able to help you maintain your lifestyle," I rattled off proudly. I loved to see my plans finally come to fruition.

Christian spat disgustedly on the floor.

"I will be the new executive producer, and you? Maybe I'll make you my personal assistant," I said, turning the knife.

"I will kill him! I will fucking kill him! And you!" Christian growled as she charged forward. She grabbed my shirt collar and pulled me in, with all of the power in her body.

I screamed, trying to fight her off.

"Christian! Please! Let her go!" Darla yelled, rushing into the dressing room. A few more staff members interceded, until finally Christian's grip loosened.

"You're finished. Your career is over," I yelled at Christian's back.

14

ON TO THE NEXT

The police stormed into Anton Barker's home office without knocking. They didn't care that they had interrupted his business meeting. Barker looked up, shock registering on his face as he stared at the many faces coming at him. The police officers didn't say a word. They didn't have to.

"If you gentlemen would excuse me," Barker said, his voice rising and falling awkwardly. The police opened a hole as the men in suits filed out of the room.

When they were all finally gone, Barker was the first to break the silence.

"Are you sure you want to do this, like this, to me?" he gritted, standing up behind his beautiful mahogany desk. "You do know who I am, right?"

"You're under arrest," one officer said, stepping forward and proceeding to read Barker his rights.

"What the hell are you talking about? I can't be under arrest. I need to call my lawyer," he said, exasperated.

He looked up and took in what was happening around him.

"Khloé . . . Mercer." Barker said my name slowly when he noticed my camera crew and me filming everything. He said my name as if he wanted each syllable to drip off of his tongue like poison. The policed reacted coolly, shoving his hands behind his back, making the scene even more television worthy. I knew him well enough now to know that would evoke a reaction.

"You just don't know what you've done, Ms. Mercer," Barker said in an eerily calm voice.

"You had people murdered. You slept with children. You robbed the city. You ruined lives, including the lives of your wife and son. You have no morals. You are not worthy of the office of mayor," I said through my teeth.

"You don't know what you've done. You just don't know," Barker continued to threaten.

"You thought you were so untouchable, but you never once thought about the city of Norfolk. You never once thought about finally receiving retribution for your evil deeds."

I couldn't hold back my tears. "All of those innocent girls will never be the same after what you did. It will take years to reunite them with their real families after suffering so many atrocities at your hands," I said as I held my head up high and proceeded to face Barker, on camera, head-on.

Barker grunted. "You'll never get away with this." He walked calmly between two police officers; they escorted him through the doorway of his office. As I followed with my live news feed, Barker's wife jumped in front of him and flattened her right hand on his chest. His eyes went round with shock. I signaled to my cameraman to zoom in so we could get every single piece of footage.

"You're going to listen, and you're going to listen good. I've taken years and years of your shit. But when your shit affects our son . . . well, that's where I draw the line," his wife gritted. "Now get on the goddamn phone and call whomever you have to call, so long as you take care of this," she spat, slapping Barker across the face with so much force, it caused him to stumble a few steps back. He didn't bother to say a word. I could tell that Barker knew by the look on his wife's face that she meant business.

At six o'clock the next morning, I climbed out of my news van, ready to watch the search and arrest warrants being executed at Detective Keith's house. After his front door went crashing in, I heard the words that were like music to my ears:

"Marlon Keith, we have a warrant for your apprehension," the first officer announced at the door.

"What? You have the wrong person. I am a cop. I work for you. This is a fucking mistake," Detective Keith said as he calmly backed up from the door and into his house. Those cops were not playing with his ass. He stumbled backward as a small army of police officers stormed into his home. Next thing he knew, he was thrown to the floor, and not so gently.

"You will have to come with us," an officer announced as he pulled Detective Keith's arms back to place handcuffs on his wrists.

"What? No! What is this? Get off of me!" he growled, frantically twisting his arms away from the officers. "I am a fucking cop! You can't do this to me! What grounds do you have for this false arrest?"

"Don't make this harder than it has to be," the arresting officer reprimanded as he loosened his grip. "We got a squirrely one here! He's resisting," the officer announced to the others. More officers rushed over.

Keith spat and bucked, like a wild hog being carried off to slaughter. It took at least five police officers to subdue him enough to get the handcuffs on him.

"You have the wrong person! Get off of me! I will have all of your jobs! Do you know who I am? Eugene Ritter, who's running for mayor of Norfolk, is my friend! Do you know that! All of you will be in the fucking unemployment line tomorrow," he screamed, all of the veins in his face and neck showing up against his skin.

"Mr. Keith, like we said at the door, we have a search warrant and an arrest warrant out for your property and you, so you need to cooperate," an officer said as he waved the paper in his face.

"Who sent you? Whoever sent you is lying! They are just trying to get back at me! This whole story was made up! I am a fucking cop! I don't know anything about what this is all about! You have to believe me!" Detective Keith continued to argue. I guess he had no intention of backing down from this fight.

"Yeah, yeah. That's what all of the people in your little organized-crime group have been saying as we've been rounding them up. You're a detective, all right, and that is why you should've known it was only going to be but so long that you could've gotten away with all the shit you were doing. We had people watching you for weeks and you never stopped. So you were a detective, but not a very smart one, apparently," the officer stated. The other officers snickered in response.

I signaled to my cameraman to zoom straight in on Detective Keith's face.

Hushed murmurs of speculation passed amongst the

nosy neighbors as they watched the commotion outside Detective Keith's house. The red, blue, and white sirens flashing in front of the sprawling mini-mansion caused quite a stir in the posh neighborhood. I was on the edge of my seat waiting for Detective Keith to emerge from his home in police custody by his own police department.

When Detective Keith, aka Redds the Killer, was escorted out in handcuffs, my heart sped up. His face was folded into an angry pout and he shouted expletives at the officers and struggled against the restraints as they shoved him into the back of the police van. Detective Keith's wife rushed out of the front door, onto their well-manicured lawn, clearly in disbelief and shock.

"They have the wrong person! Tell them! All of you know me!" he shouted at his neighbors as he was brought through the door. They all quickly turned their faces and averted their eyes, pretending not to hear or see.

Detective Keith stepped up to the van. Before he was loaded into the back, he spotted me standing nearby with a WXOT-TV microphone in my hand and a camera crew at my side. I winked and smirked at his ass.

"You bitch! You lying little bitch! I know this was all of your doing! You were the same one who set up Barker! You won't get away with this! I swear that when I get out, I will be coming straight for you!" he threatened.

I laughed out loud as I watched the officers force Detective Keith into the waiting van. "Have fun living in a prison," I mumbled under my breath.

I took even greater satisfaction in knowing that all of the media vehicles, including the WXOT-TV van, were on the scene to cover the arrest. I didn't even mind sharing this moment with other stations.

Detective Keith was finally getting what was coming to

him. I could just imagine what all of the story headlines would read: DIRTY DETECTIVE BUSTED FOR DEALING DRUGS; DRUG-DEALING DETECTIVE PREYED ON VULNERABLE STREET CRIMINALS; DRUG SCANDAL HITS NORFOLK POLICE DEPARTMENT.

I smiled. "Well, all-mighty Detective Keith, looks like someone else was doing the investigating this time?" I quipped, pointing to myself. "And it wasn't even as complicated as you police make it seem," I continued, speaking to myself and pointing out of the window at the police car holding Detective Keith.

"I hope you see a lot of friends in prison. I'm sure the ones you put away illegally can't wait to make your acquaintance," I said, hitting my thigh as I laughed out loud.

"Next time do your job and what the taxpayers pay you to do!" I spat as if Detective Keith could hear me. With that, I took position at the right camera angle. I headed toward the big spectacle of police cars and vans. At this point I was going to see the case against Barker, Keith, and all of the rest of the major players all the way through, which even meant picking some of these killers out of a lineup as the people who'd committed murders and trafficked innocent children.

"You guys ready to go?" I asked, turning to my crew with a smile. This was the biggest story I covered since I had bested Christian and gotten my co-camera job at WXOT-TV.

"In five, four, three, two," my own personal cameraman counted down before we went live with the story:

"In breaking news we are outside the home of Detective Marlon Keith, a dangerous criminal who doubled as a police detective. Our investigation revealed that Keith participated in at least twelve murders over the past four years as he worked for former criminal defense attorney turned crime boss Anton Barker. It is reported that Keith, during those four years, worked as a legitimate police detective, but was really a ruthless criminal enforcer who tortured and killed at the will of the mayoral candidate Anton Barker. As you can see here, Detective Keith is being transported to jail by his own Norfolk Police Department.

"The department is reportedly ashamed that one of their own would engage in such criminal acts," said the chief of the Norfolk Police Department. Our investigation uncovered that former Detective Keith helped Barker engage in drug dealing, cold-blooded murder, illegal gambling rings, and, worst of all, child sex trafficking. Neighbors say they were shocked to learn that the neighbor that they had known as the best detective in the city of Norfolk for his one hundred percent solve rate, was not actually who he had claimed to be. Thanks to the protection of high-up government officials and other corrupt politicians, Keith was able to successfully assume the double identity that he held for so many years. He reportedly successfully ruined the careers of several upstanding former police officers who had started to figure out Keith's dirty deeds and threatened to blow the whistle on Keith and all of the other corrupt government officials in office in the city of Norfolk.

"Earlier today one of the innocent police officers that Keith had framed for misconduct, and later fired for speaking out against Keith, had this to say . . .

" 'We are just truly blessed and grateful that Detective Keith did not have a chance to do more damage or hurt any more people during the time he was out on the street. Our group of officers in solidarity against corruption would like to thank Khloé Mercer and WXOT-TV for all of their help in getting to the bottom of this organized-crime ring. Now we are just hoping to move on with our lives in peace and get what is owed to us after all of this time.'

"Thank you, I am sure everyone involved is breathing a sigh of relief. Reporting for WXOT-TV, I am Khloé Mercer."

15

BACK TO HAUNT ME

I had been sleeping much better with Barker and Keith behind bars. My reporting on the story didn't stop at them. I had continued and at least six more dudes had gone down as part of their organized-crime ring.

I was knocked out cold when I heard it. I groaned and slapped at my nightstand for my phone. As soon as I cracked my eyes open, pain rocked through my skull.

"Fuck," I hissed, finally locating my phone. "Hello," I grumbled, my own breath threatening to kill me.

"Khloé!"

Ugh, I moved the phone from my ear quickly. My head was pounding too hard for the damn screaming.

"Khloé! You there?" I could hear Liza even with the phone away from my ear. I had never heard her speak so loudly. She and I had become as close as best friends after everything we did together for the story.

"Liza, what the hell? Why are you screaming like that?" I rasped. My voice was heavy with sleep. I had sat up and binge watched a whole season of some new show the night before. Finally giving myself some time and a break away from being at work all day, every day. I had told myself I needed a break after all I had been through, so this was supposed to be my time to relax—and Liza knew that.

"You better start talking fast. I don't take too kindly to being woken up like this," I grumped at her.

"Girl, listen to me! Somebody just came to the news station and told the chief that you have been nominated for a News and Documentary Emmy Award! They haven't announced it yet, but it's you! You were nominated, and you got the station nominated, too, for your story!" Liza yelled.

I sucked my teeth. She had to be crazy and mistaken, either that or she was pranking me.

"Liza, I am trying to get some much-needed rest. Today is not the day for jokes and pranks, especially not like this."

"No! I am not kidding, Khloé. I would not joke about something as serious as this. I'm telling you, it is you. I heard it with my own ears. This is not a dream. This is not a joke. You are awake and talking to me, and you are fucking nominated for an Emmy Award!" Liza went on with so much excitement, I was all the way awake now.

I finally sat up, scrubbed my hands over my face, and wiped the sleep out of my eyes.

"Well? Khloé? Do you believe me now?" Liza asked.

"Umm. Yes. But I don't know what to say or do. I am sitting here in shock or something like that. I don't even know whether to get up, jump up and down, scream, or just sit here and let this shit sink into my brain," I said, looking out into my apartment like someone was going to appear and tell me this was all a dream and I was still asleep.

"Girl, I'll be there in twenty minutes to help you figure out what to do. You must be crazy, it is time to celebrate," Liza said before hanging right up on me.

Liza was not playing. As soon as I stepped out of the shower, I had just enough time to wrap myself in my terry cloth robe before she was pounding on my door.

"Oh, my God, this girl," I mumbled as I padded to the door. I snatched the door open and Liza rushed inside so fast, a swift wind passed my face from her movement.

"Okay, let's start with, what are you going to wear to the awards?" Liza huffed out of breath, wasting no ass time as she rushed into my place.

"Um, hello to you too," I said, shaking my head at her. "Damn. You're more excited than me. I don't think this has settled into my brain yet."

"Girl, you know I love you already. We don't have to waste time. I'm telling you, girl, you are a star now. This is what you have been working for. This is the best revenge against Christian, even better than you winning her job and pushing her ass the hell out," Liza said. She was damn near cheering; she was so loud and excited.

"Liza, this is so unbelievable. But you know I don't take pleasure in doing anything to Christian, she brought all of that on herself with the way she was. I say it was all karma on her ass," I corrected.

Liza waved her hand in front of her face. "That's beside the point. Damn it, you need to make sure you're going to look stunning and fabulous for the awards. You have a few weeks, I know that, but this is way too exciting to just sit still about it."

Of course, I was going to make sure I looked stunning. I had literally been working toward this my whole entire life. I was trying to play it cool for Liza, when, in actuality, my insides were jumping so badly, I thought my lungs would come up out of my mouth. I moved around my apartment to get dressed so I could go to the station and get the official word from the powers that be. I grabbed the purse I carried all the time, because I called it my lucky purse. I turned toward Liza who couldn't even keep still. She looked at me through wide eyes.

"Are you ready for the biggest day, well, aside from the day of the awards and the day you got those criminals put away—oh, and the day you were born—but, anyway, one of the biggest days of your life?" Liza asked, rambling in that fast, quavery voice she always spoke in when she was either nervous or excited. I was getting used to it. Her energy was contagious, though. I couldn't help but catch the bug and be super excited too.

My heart sped up. She and I were both thinking the same thing, and we both opened our mouths at the same time.

"I hope you . . ."

"I hope you . . ."

"Always stay close to me," we said in unison.

Liza rushed into me and we hugged for a long moment. I returned her embrace. She was a genuine soul, for real, and I was glad I had become friends with her.

"Let's go get the good news from the horse's mouth," I said.

"Yes! Yes! Yes!" Liza waved her hands frantically. "Oh, my God."

It was good to see how happy Liza was for me, especially since I told her that I'd give her some of the credit for this blockbuster story. I told her that if I won, she won too.

"I don't know how I will react," I said, trying to imagine what I'd do when they told me firsthand, I had been nominated.

"Girl, do whatever that big brain of yours tells you to do, including jump up on the station chief's desk and shake your ass like a crazy person," Liza joked.

"I can't do that, because then they'd have my ass committed to the psych ward and I'd miss the entire awards show," I joked back.

We had a good laugh. All the way to the news station, we tried to make small talk, but everything always led back to the nomination and award. I wanted to get the official word before I decided to call Kyle and my mother. Kyle had been checking in with me more regularly since the story broke than he'd ever done before.

I walked into the station and all eyes were on me. I held my head up high, with my chin jutting forward, like I was a star. I looked at each and every person who looked at me. Some smiled and nodded; others glared and whispered. That was fine with me. I knew jealousy still ran rampant up in WXOT. There was a bunch of Christian's people that I had removed, once I took over her job. I also hired more minorities again. It was great to see the tables turn up in there. Liza was hovering next to me like a bee to honey. I don't even think she realized that her ass was jogging alongside me like a crazy person.

"Just breathe and keep your head held high. You got this, Khloé," Liza urged.

I turned to her right before I knocked on the station chief's door. "Who knew that a little girl from the hood, whose father was murdered in front of her, and whose mother battled back from the worst drug addiction ever, could turn out like this? Who knew I'd end up taking down a crime syndicate and being considered for an Emmy Award in the process, which was all in a day's work for me? Who knew, Liza?" I said on the verge of happy tears.

Liza swiped at the tears on her face too. It was so easy to make her cry.

"You knew . . . that's who," Liza said, pumping her fist triumphantly.

I swear, between the still-lingering remnants of that interrupted sleep and the excitement of what was about to come, I almost had a damn heart attack. I actually had to clutch my damn chest to keep myself from fainting and spilling onto the floor.

"Okay. Okay," Liza huffed, fanning herself with one hand and clutching the nominee invite card with the other hand. "I have the numbers. We have the tickets. How we going to do this?" She was huffing and puffing like she was about to hyperventilate. "Girl, go into that office. You are taking too long to get that official word. I can't take the buildup another minute. Got me all riled up," Liza said, flustered.

I knocked on the chief's door, waited for a few seconds, and pushed my way inside. He was sitting behind his desk like the king of the hill. No one ever really came to see him, and the last time I'd been there was when he told me I had done a damn good job on my story and had landed Christian's job.

"Ah, Khloé, I was expecting you," the chief said, smiling with his old, ugly yellow teeth showing.

I swear, I think that man never went home or left that office. He looked as if his life was all contained in this space.

"Okay," I replied. Then I blew out a breath and sat down. I closed my eyes and took a deep breath and waited for him to drop the news on me. "Thank you for having me come up."

"So, first, your story caused quite a stir around here, as you already know," he said. "It was probably the single most important piece of news reporting we have ever done here at WXOT. I appreciated that," the chief said.

I felt a warm feeling explode inside me. I loved being in his good graces. Now I kind of understood why Christian loved being in her job so much. It felt good to have others look at you in a good way.

"With that being said," the chief went on.

I gripped the sides of the chair until my knuckles ached. I blew out an exasperated breath.

"I am proud to tell you . . ." He was dragging the shit out.

"Go ahead," I urged, moving to the edge of the chair, still holding on for dear life.

"You, Khloé Mercer, have been . . ."

I was silent, because suddenly, as I sat there waiting for the words to leave his ugly, wrinkled mouth, my stomach knotted so badly, I had the urge to double over, but didn't.

"You have been nominated for . . ." He leaned into his desk so far, his old neck jiggled.

I swallowed hard. "Ye . . . yeah, I . . . um . . ."

"The very prestigious News and Documentary Emmy Awards for 2020," the chief finally relayed, his voice going up higher than I'd ever heard it go. I guess that was his version of excited.

"Wh-what?" I asked, barely able to speak, as if I didn't already know about it. I closed my eyes and waited to hear him say the rest. Everything in the room was spinning off axis, and, trust me, it wasn't the fear this time.

"Oh, my God!" I screamed, jumping up out of the chair. I lost all good sense and sensibilities at that time. Although Liza had already told me, I didn't realize how the realization of what I'd accomplished hadn't hit me yet.

"I can't believe it!" I started bouncing on my knees and fanning my hands in front of myself. I swear, I felt like my soul had left my body. I don't know how else to describe the crazy out-of-body experience I had in that moment.

"Ms. Mercer, thank you for your hard work and bringing this very wanted attention to our little local news station. It is not every day that this happens for small newscasts like ours," the chief went on, as if anything he said was going to stick in my head at that moment.

I couldn't speak. I stared at the chief, waiting for him to finish, while trying to control my trembling hands.

"This is the official golden nomination certificate for your keepsake," he said, extending the small sparkly, golden card toward me.

"Thank you," I said, grabbing it, turning on my heels, and almost running out of the office.

As soon as I stepped into the hallway, Liza was there. "Khloé! Let me see!" Liza urged frantically.

I held out my quaking hand. Liza snatched the card and examined it for a few seconds.

"Agh!" She belted out the most ear-shattering scream I'd ever heard. Her scream snapped me out of my catatonic shock. I jumped so hard, I almost fell back into the wall.

"Oh, my God!" I screeched, and, believe it or not, I jumped so high off the floor, I know the staff at the station might've thought someone was chasing me or beating my ass. I continued to jump up and down too. Liza and I jumped and hugged and screamed and cried and danced and went round and round, until we were finally exhausted and almost collapsed to the floor, heaving and out of breath.

"Girl," Liza gasped out the word, barely able to gather enough breath.

"Girrrrlllllllll," I dragged mine out on a long breath,

hardly able to breathe myself. "Agh!" I screamed, and flailed my arms in the air.

Liza turned her head and looked over at me, straight on. "Agh!" she screamed too, and flailed her arms the same way. We busted out laughing. It was the kind of laughter that said we were set for life and would never have another care in the world. I had hit the news world lottery all from bringing down Anton Barker and his crew! My mother always said that it was better to be born lucky than rich!

16

THE FAÇADE OF HAPPINESS

I spun around like a fairy tale princess. I was so full of joy inside. I had finally made it. I had finally gotten what I wanted after every single struggle I'd endured.

All of my life I knew I was going to be successful. There was no doubt in my mind that I'd make it big one day. Being a successful news anchor was the only thing I'd dreamed about since I was a kid. My mother, God bless her heart, wasn't the best example, but she overcame her demons and was waiting at home to watch and cheer me on. I didn't have many strong-woman examples in my life, but my father, before he died, had helped me come up with a mantra: *I am strong, beautiful, successful, and wonderfully made.* I had hammered that into my little mind from the time I could say the alphabet.

"Khloé Dawn Mercer," my father would say, calling me by my whole government name. "You're so smart. You're so pretty. Those big hazel eyes and that sandy brown hair are going to get you the best spot on TV. You watch! You're going to be a go getter and a head turner when you grow up."

I'd always believed every word he'd said too. There was something special about me. Not to brag, I just always knew and felt it inside me.

All through high school I obsessed over doing well in school with the one goal in mind. I never partied or went out, like my brother did. And I certainly didn't stop striving to move forward. At that point I had overcome a lot of tragedy and struggle, and I was determined to make a life for myself—a good life, that is.

Now, standing inside the grand foyer of the hotel, fingers curled so tightly into my palms that my knuckles turned white, with my heart punching against my chest wall, I waited for my date and prepared myself to walk the red carpet of the News and Documentary Emmy Awards. This was like life coming full circle. My story reporting had gained me an Emmy nomination, something that was not an easy task either. Who knows what's going to come at me tomorrow? I can't say. But I can say that I'm gonna relish in this moment now and think about tomorrow when it gets here.

I'd already given myself five pep talks about how I should react if I didn't win. I'd told myself there would be another time. I'd told myself I would win and give my speech like a pro. I'd told myself I would not cry. Still, nothing I told myself eased the electric currents of nervousness coursing through my body. I swallowed hard so that my sparkly diamond choker rose and fell against the ladder of my throat. I would've paced in circles, if I didn't have on thirty-minute heels.

"We are almost ready for you," the red-carpet organizer said, patting my shoulder. She smiled warmly and I returned the favor.

I nodded and shifted my weight from one foot to the other, balancing carefully on my sparkly Christian Louboutin pumps. I'd gone all out for the occasion. It wouldn't have been right if I hadn't. I mean for me, this was a once-in-a-lifetime experience. It was nearly unheard of for a small local television station, like the one I worked at, to have a story so good, so newsworthy, that the station and I got nominated for an Emmy.

"You have made us proud," my bosses at the station had said. That was like the proudest moment of my life, given the fact that I'd been under the gun for a good story.

"Are you ready?"

I startled. I blinked a few times and looked to my right. I smiled.

"I guess so," I replied, jamming my right fist into my hip and bending my arm at the elbow to make an opening for my brother, Kyle, to slide his arm through.

"You look amazing, pretty eyes," Kyle said, his voice deep.

My stomach clenched. My father had always called me that when I was little. "Hey, pretty eyes."

A small explosion of heat lit in my chest as I thought about my father not being here through everything we'd been through over the years. I silently wished he had been around. There were so many things I wanted to tell him, and I wanted to say so many things to my father.

I closed my eyes and exhaled. I shook my head, wishing away my worries. I couldn't focus on the past right now. If I did, I might not make it down the red carpet without mascara all over my face. And I couldn't have that. I had to look perfect for this occasion.

"You clean up nicely yourself," I replied to my brother, smiling so hard my cheeks hurt.

Just then, I heard the low hum of the music that invited the next round of guests out onto the X in the center of the red carpet. That was my signal.

Kyle squared his shoulders and tightened his lock on my

arm so that I was forced a little closer to him. "A'ight, twin, here we go. On TV and shit. This is type crazy."

I blew out a long breath. "I know, right? And I would have no other date but you, because without you this story wouldn't have been possible," I said in return.

"That was a small thing," he replied.

I looked down and smoothed my left hand over the fine, hand-sewn beads on the front of my floor-length couture gown. I tensed up and got ready to walk out in front of throngs of people and tons of paparazzi. There was a quick, fleeting thought in my mind that the crowd might have some people in it that weren't happy about my story reporting. But I quickly let those invasive thoughts pass.

"Loosen up," Kyle said. "You've been working for this all of your life, right? And we here now, so you can't go running and hiding. We here now, twin."

I parted a quivery-lipped smile. "The way I'm shaking, you'd think I was hosting the show or something. All I've got to do is make it past these cameras and get to my seat—that is, unless I win."

"You mean *when* you win," Kyle corrected lovingly. He was the best.

I sucked in my breath as we finally stood at the end of the beautifully decorated red carpet outside the Microsoft Theater in downtown L.A. The scene was magic. Lights flashing. Gorgeous people and celebrities flowing down the red carpet taking their turns stopping and letting others take pictures of them. The stars were being interviewed about their outfits and who'd designed them while the paparazzi were taking pictures. My heart was racing, but in a good way. It was a dream come true out there.

With my arm hooked through my brother's, I plastered on a smile and in my heels carefully navigated the thick red carpet. Collective awestruck gasps rose and fell amongst the crowd standing on either side of the decorated path. But it was the glares and smirks from four men in suits that had caused me to stumble a bit. I noticed them right away; they were clearly not there to celebrate. I was a long way from Norfolk, where I'd broken my story and busted up some pretty dangerous people's lives.

Maybe I'm just being paranoid, I thought. Everyone had been taken down, back in Norfolk, so it was impossible they'd sent people to L.A. And to the Emmy Awards of all places! I couldn't stop to tell Kyle about my paranoia, or suspicions—whichever way you wanted to look at it. He was too busy smiling and waving, as if he were the one who had been nominated. Stopping to tell him something serious would have messed up the pictures we were having snapped of us. I continued to smile and play it off like I hadn't noticed the men.

Focus, Khloé, focus. Those guys are probably just security. But somewhere deep down inside, I had a strong feeling those men were there to make a point about what had happened after my story broke. Their presence was like a threat whispered in my ear.

It'll all be over soon. Then I can move on and maybe stay in L.A. and never return to Norfolk, I spoke to myself.

Kyle stepped to the side to let me get a few pictures alone. Just like me, he wore a smile that said, *I'm proud.* Unlike my big fancy gown, with all the sparkles and expensive sparkly shoes, my brother was simple. He wore a plain black suit instead of a fancy tuxedo. He had argued me down about wearing a tux. I'd finally given up.

"Ms. Mercer! Ms. Mercer! Over here," a paparazzo cameraman called out to me. Then another and another.

I am really famous now. Wow!

I felt something flutter inside. With everything I'd been

through, I had lost sight of how rewarding my job really was. Just then, one of the red-carpet reporters rushed over to me with her microphone jutting out in front of her.

"Ms. Mercer, who are you wearing tonight?" she asked.

I blushed and twirled around so she could get a better look. "I'm wearing Michael Costello, custom-made," I gushed.

"Beautiful. So tell us, the story that got you here, you put your life in danger, correct?" the reporter asked boldly.

A cold feeling came over me for a second. I dropped my smile just thinking back on it.

"Well, any good reporter sometimes has to do things to get the real story," I came back at her.

"Even if it means a bit of selling your soul," she asked, pushing her microphone right to my lips.

"Thank you for your time," I replied, annoyed. I grabbed Kyle, took one last look over my shoulder for those men, and headed inside.

The awards seemed to drag on. By the time they'd gotten to the category I was nominated in, I was completely filled with anxiety.

"And the nominees for Outstanding Coverage of a Breaking News Story are . . ."

I clenched my butt cheeks together and balled up my toes in my shoes so hard that they throbbed.

Kyle reached over and grabbed my hand and held it tightly.

I closed my eyes and waited to hear the results. My ears were ringing so loudly from my nerves that I didn't hear anything until cheers erupted from the crowd.

"You won, twin! They just called your name! You won," Kyle blurted loudly. He beamed with pride. It took me a few minutes to register what he was saying. He let go of my hand and helped me to my feet. My mouth hung open in a perfectly round O, and my legs were shaking so badly that my knees knocked together. I could barely catch my breath, and that instinctive right hand over my heart told the whole story.

"You have to go up there," Kyle said, urging me into the aisle so I could walk onstage and get my award.

Kyle held on to me to make sure I could balance on my heels; I guess he could feel how hard I was trembling. He walked me up onto the stage. I stood frozen for a few seconds as I turned toward the spectators. Cheers arose. My cheeks flushed and the bones in my face ached from grinning. I deserved this Emmy Award. At least that was what the loud crowd was saying with their warm cheers.

I looked over at my brother, and he wore a cool grin as I slowly unfolded the paper containing my speech. I wish I could've been as cool as he was in that moment. My hands shook, but I stuck out my chest and delivered the perfect speech to accept my award. The crowd clapped and cheered again as Kyle and I walked toward the stage exit.

"Wait right there . . . hold that pose!" a photographer called out. "Smile, you're the winner," he instructed, hoisting his camera to eye level to ensure he captured the exact moment. I was blushing and sure that my face would look like a cherry in every snapshot he took.

Kyle and I posed and turned to each other on cue. We capitalized on the opportunity to take this free twin-sister-and-brother photo shoot. The photographer's flash exploded.

The bright lights sparkled in my eyes. It was truly the perfect day in my life.

"Walk slowly forward now," the photographer instructed. When Kyle and I finally made it to the end of the picture area, I was bombarded with more photographers eager to snap photos with professional and personal cameras. Noticing the paparazzi, even Kyle waved like a star. I also flashed my best debutante smile.

"Well, well, well. If it isn't the great reporter . . ." A tall man in a suit stepped into our path, clapping his hand on my shoulder. My smile faded and I bit down into my jaw.

"I didn't think you'd go through with showing up here, all out in the public. We're all proud of you back in Norfolk. You still got a lot of balls," he said, smiling wickedly, the bright stage lights glinting off his one gold tooth.

He turned his attention to Kyle. "You can thank your sister for everything."

I shivered.

"Ms. Mercer!" another photographer shouted, jutting his camera forward for a close-up. I twisted away from the man in the suit, happy for the distraction. Kyle and I hurried down the walkway, faking happiness so we didn't make a scene. It didn't last for long.

"Khloé! Khloé Mercer!" a male voice boomed.

My head jerked at the voice. Still smiling and faking like I wasn't about to faint from fear, I turned to my right.

"You should've stayed the fuck out of the way! You fucked with the wrong people!" the voice boomed again. The source barreled through the crowd, heading straight toward Kyle and me.

"Gun! He's got a gun!" a lady photographer screamed first.

"Oh, shit!" Kyle's eyes went round as he faced the long metal nose of the weapon. Frantically he unhooked his arm from mine and stepped in front of me. Before he could make another move, the sound of rapid-fire explosions cut through the air.

The entire place went crazy. The hired security seemed to materialize out of the walls and began running at full speed, guns drawn. Things were going crazy. Photographers, cameramen, backstage staff . . . everyone was running in a million directions. Two of the security guards were picked off, falling to the floor like knocked-over bowling pins. Screams pierced the air from every direction.

Kyle's body jerked from being hit with bullets. He was snatched from my side in an instant. I turned and watched as my brother's arms flew up, bent at the elbow and flailing like a puppet on a string. His body crumpled like a rag doll and fell into an awkward heap on the floor, right at my feet. It was all too familiar.

There was no way I could lose my brother in this way. Not after everything. I stood frozen; my feet were seemingly rooted into the floor under me. This was just a bad dream. It wasn't real. I couldn't get enough air into my lungs to breathe.

"Kyle!" I shrieked, finally finding my voice.

"Help!" someone yelled. "Call the police! Help!" More screams erupted around us.

The sounds of people screaming and loud booms exploded around me. I coughed as the grainy, metallic grit of gunpowder settled at the back of my throat. I inched forward on the floor next to Kyle. The smell of bloody raw meat wafted up my nose. The floor around him had pooled into a deep red pond of blood. Everything was happening so fast. I blinked my eyes to make sure this was real.

"Kyle!" I screamed so loud that my throat burned. I grabbed his shoulders and shook them, hoping for a response.

"No!" I sobbed, throwing my body on top of his. I just knew I wasn't out of danger. I knew who it was they wanted, and it was me.

More deafening booms blasted through the air.

I couldn't think as I lay on the floor. The thundering footfalls of fleeing guests left me feeling abandoned and adrift. I lay next to Kyle, listening to his labored breathing.

"Why? How did we let this happen? How did we get here?" I sobbed. "How did this all happen?"

"Hey! You've got to get out of here," a security guard huffed, pulling me up onto my feet. I was shocked to see that I hadn't been hit. "Get out of here. Run as fast as you can and hide," he instructed. He hurled demands as fast as his lips could spew them out.

"I . . . can't . . . leave . . ."

"I'll take care of him as best I can, but it doesn't make sense for you both to die," the guard told me. "Now run!"

17

THE RECKONING

I hitched up my dress and did as I was told. I ran out the side door he'd pointed to and took off like someone had put wings on my back. The wind whipped over my face so hard, it snatched my breath. My tongue felt like it would disintegrate as my breath came out so hard and fast that it made the inside of my mouth desert dry. If I didn't know any better, I would've thought I was having a heart attack. My chest heaved up and down, and my shirt stuck to my sweat-slicked skin.

I still couldn't believe I was in this situation, and all for what? For a good story? For a better position at a job that didn't give a damn about anything, but getting the story first? I was risking my life and limb. I had literally been selling my soul to please them.

"Agh!" A scream unconsciously escaped my mouth when I realized the footsteps thundering behind me were closing in. A flash of panic caused me to almost double over and dry heave.

"Oh, my God," I gasped, eyeing the path ahead of me

filled with people and cars and all sorts of things that were in my way. As my feet pounded the concrete, and my body moved forward like a charging bull's, I could see people either jumping out of my way or stopping and watching the drama unfold. One thing was sure, no one was going to stop and intervene. Society was different now—people ran away from any signs of danger, not sure if they'd be innocently pulled in and possibly killed or not. I knew there was no chance of me having a chivalrous stranger pop out and help me. No chance at all.

I panted and whipped my head around frantically. I peered quickly over my shoulder, trying to see how much time I had left, how far of a distance I had gotten away. My eyes went wide at what I saw. They were closing in on me fast. My pursuers were right there. They were weaving through the throngs of people on the street to get me.

"Shit!" I swallowed hard, listening to the commotions from footsteps behind me progress from rapid taps to gallops. I turned around one more time, which was a mistake. More rapid footsteps closed in behind me. They were hot on my heels.

Moving my body around in terror, I saw the shadowy silhouette of a monstrous figure. I knew it was him: the killer. He was gaining on me. I had no choice. I lifted my aching legs and forged ahead like my life depended on it, which it did.

With raggedy, jagged puffs of air escaping my lips, I ducked down a side street and looked around for a hiding place. I ran to a row of Dumpsters. Knowing they'd look there first, I passed it and dived behind a tall wall of industrial-sized garbage bags. I buried myself under them and lay perfectly still, hoping they wouldn't find me. Hoping he wouldn't sniff me out. They always said, killers have an instinct and they can smell fear. As I lay in that pile of bags, the strong smell of rotting garbage and shit shot up into my nostrils. I didn't care. It was either inhale the stench, or die. I chose the nasty odor in exchange for my life. Chills covered my body. I clenched my lips together tightly, trying to slow the sound of my panting and keep my teeth from chattering so loudly.

After a few seconds of hiding, I heard something scratching next to me. I squinted my eyes to see where the noise was coming from. It seemed to be getting closer and closer. The scratching sound was growing louder and louder. I shifted a little bit and finally I could see the source of the noise.

A rat! Oh, my God!

I was deathly afraid of rats. I felt my bladder fill up and suddenly I felt like I would pee myself. My first instinct was to move, until suddenly I peeked and noticed the shiny black shoes of one of the men chasing me. I could hear the others slamming the covers of the Dumpsters and murmuring to each other as they searched. I heard one of them cock a gun. An involuntary whimper bubbled up to my lips. I quickly put my hand up to my mouth. My body trembled fiercely. Then, to make matters worse, the rat moved over my legs. This time a tiny bit of pee leaked from my bladder. The nasty critter moved slowly at first, and when I jerked to get it off of me, it began to run over my body. I swear, I almost died five times.

Desperate to get it off of me, I shook my leg harder this time, but that just scared it and made the rat crawl up my torso toward my face. I began to hyperventilate, and tears ran out of my eyes. The rat was heading straight for my face. Now, not only was I being chased by killers, who wanted to end my life, but I was about to be bitten by a nasty rat and would probably get some disease that would kill me anyway. The rat got to my neck and all hell broke loose then. I panicked and instinctively lifted my hands to swat it away. It hissed at me, flashed its beady red eyes, and bared its jagged teeth. That was it. The fear snatched all my good senses and I screamed. That spooked the rat and it ran up my face, over my head, and jumped down and away.

I quickly clasped both of my hands over my mouth right after, but I was sure it was too late. Sweat trickled down my face and burned my eyes. My heart jackhammered against my chest bone so hard, it actually hurt. My stomach knotted up so tightly, the cramps were almost unbearable.

"She's over there, here!" I heard one of the goons scream to the others. The next thing I heard was their rapid footfalls. It was over now. I was a dead woman. I swallowed hard and started praying under my breath. I decided in that moment that I wasn't going out without a fight. I pushed the big bags off of me to free myself so I could try to run again. I couldn't believe I had risked it all for a story. Everything I had worked for had come down to this moment—a moment I might not survive.

"You're about to die, bitch!" I heard one say as soon as I freed myself.

I was back off and running, but I didn't get too far.

Bang!

The ear-shattering sound of a gunshot was the last thing I remember . . .

I came into consciousness to voices talking around me. "Look, this is definitely the girl who did all of the damage," I heard a man insist.

"I am not letting her get away this time. You just need to be on board," the man growled. I felt myself being hoisted up at that moment. I swear, my heart seized in my chest. I thought I was dead before, but now I knew I wasn't.

"Get off of me!" I yelled. Just then, a black van screeched

to a halt in front of us. The strange man smiled wickedly. Three men jumped out of the van. They pushed me toward them.

"What the fuck," I huffed, my eyes going wide. I looked around me with desperation dancing over my face. It was too late. These people meant business, and it was clear that the promises and threats that had been made against me were going to be carried out.

"Who are you?! Who the fuck are you?!" I screamed as I whipped my head around.

"Your worst fucking nightmare," another man said evenly. One of the men from the van threw a black bag over my head, while the other two forced me, kicking and screaming, into the van.

"Take her to the warehouse," one of them said. "Pick up the stuff that she dropped, the earring and bracelet. We can't leave any clues of her disappearance behind. There will be no saving her this time."

"Yes, sir, boss," the driver of the van answered.

Lying on the cold, metal floor of the van, I kicked and moved my body frantically.

"Keep fucking still, before I tie your ass up," one of the men growled at me.

"Fuck you," I spat.

A huge, booted foot slammed into my ribs. "Agh!" I cried out. I coughed, but I kept trying to fight. A punch landed to my face and I saw stars, but I still didn't stop fighting. Another one of the men got close to me and tried to get me tied up. I moved so much, the black hood covering my head came up slightly, but the man didn't see it in time.

"Agh!" the man belted out.

I had clamped my teeth down on his wrist and wouldn't let go.

"Get the fuck off of me, bitch!" he hollered.

I thrust my foot forward and caught the other man in the balls.

"Ooof!" he wheezed, rolling over onto his side.

"What the fuck is going on back there?!" the driver screamed.

I released my bite on the first man's wrist and blood covered my mouth. I struggled to get up, but the man I had kicked in the balls recovered and moved toward me.

"You dead now, bitch," he hissed, obviously still reeling from the pain. I squirmed helplessly. I had no more tricks left, especially with the constraints of that fancy gown I had on. Both men were well aware of what they were dealing with now. In pain and a little dazed, I tried to roll as far away from them as I could. I was too slow, and there was nowhere for me to run. The man I had bitten kneeled over me and lifted his gun . . . and *Bam!* Blackness came down on me with quickness.

When I regained consciousness, I heard the muffled sound of voices surrounding me. The pounding in my head was so bad, even my teeth hurt.

"Mmm," I groaned, trying in vain to lift my hand to shield my eyes from the bright lights.

"She's awake!" a man announced loudly.

"Good. Bring her over here so she can see the mess she's made," another man's voice echoed loudly through the hollowed room.

"Ahh," I winced. Pain shot through my rib cage as I was handled roughly. I was dragged to another part of the expansive warehouse. Before I could see it, the smell hit me like a kick in the chest and I gagged. It was a mixture of raw meat gone bad, burning flesh, shit, and piss.

"You know him?" one of the men asked, grabbing a

handful of my hair and forcing my downturned head upward.

"No. No!" I shook my head in denial as tears raced down my bruised cheeks. "Kyle," I rasped. They had snatched my brother from the theater and had him in this place. I couldn't even look at Kyle's naked and bleeding body suspended by chains from a metal rafter. There was a piece of metal that resembled a horse bit forced with wires hanging from between Kyle's lips. I knew there was no way he would make it through this.

"Oh, so you do know him," the man said, amused. He nodded at his henchmen. One of them walked over to a small box that contained three levers. He flipped on the switches and pulled down the first lever.

"Grrrr! Grrrr! Agh!" I screamed as I watched Kyle's body jerk and curl in response to the high jolts of electricity that hit him. I heard some kind of liquid splashing on the floor and knew it was coming from my brother's dying body.

"Please! No! Stop!" I begged, closing my eyes.

The man let out a raucous, maniacal laugh. I kept my eyes closed and my head down. The lead torturer signaled his men to cut the electricity. Kyle's body finally relaxed, but it swung limp and lifeless above my head.

"One more round of that and he won't make it," the man said, smiling evilly at me. "He was the one who showed you around inside our organization, didn't he? Isn't that sweet of your brother? All that time of you sneaking around inside our operations, he was the entire reason you were able to. We couldn't figure out who had been the mole inside. Then, just like that, I find out you were related to him. It was right under my nose," he continued cruelly. "You know what's worse than a snitch? A traitor. And what is worse than a traitor? A coward like this."

"Let him go," I croaked through my battered lips. "It's me you want. Not him. Not them. I'm here. I'm not scared to die. Just let him go and kill me!"

"I'll get to that, but first, I want you to see what if feels like to have those close to you suffer for no reason," the man gritted. "Now open your fucking eyes and look at him before I gut him like a pig, just like what happened to your father!"

I slowly lifted my head with fire flashing in my eyes. My hands involuntarily curled into fists. I looked up at Kyle's limp and badly abused body.

"I'm sorry, twin," I whispered. With that, the electricity was turned on again and Kyle's body bucked fiercely. At first, he didn't make any sounds, but then I heard low growling coming from his mouth. I thought he was already dead.

"Wait! Stop! I have some information about your boss and the things he did behind your backs," I screamed out. "You can kill me after, but let my brother go!"

The man laughed again. "There is nothing you can tell me about my boss—except you decided you put him away for a long time and now I have been commissioned to exact revenge," he growled, getting close to me and grabbing a fistful of my hair.

"He . . . he was doing things behind your back," I whispered through my swollen lips.

"What?" the man hissed.

"He was making side deals because he strongly believed that he was going to become mayor and side with the feds to boost his run for governor and eventually president," I told him. The man released his grasp on my hair with a shove. I fell forward and hit my face on the concrete floor. The pain sent a flash of anger through my entire body. I got up onto my knees and fell back down from my legs being so weak. I didn't give up; I pushed myself up again.

I would rather die on my feet than live on my knees, I said to myself. Those were words my father had always said to Kyle and me.

"He was raping little girls. He participated in the abuse of children. He hated you and said he only did business with your dirty Mexican ass because he wanted money and security. The things he couldn't do for himself, and the people he wanted out of his way, he used you for that," I said, still struggling to get to my feet.

"What the fuck are you talking about?" the man snarled, his nostrils flaring. He could feel the gazes of his men bearing down on him. I could see everyone looking for the next fact I was going to drop.

"Him—that one right there, who worked with your so-called boss—he was part of it all. The time the shipment went missing . . . he planned it all out. They were planning on doing your ass dirty and running off together, but not before they made sure you went down. All of the proof is right here in my head. I saw it all as I gathered the story. I have no reason to lie, and how would I know who worked with who! Him . . . he was lying and is still lying," I growled. I got to my feet. I swayed unsteadily, but at least I was able to look him in the eyes.

Within ten minutes they dragged the other guy over and stood him up in front of the leader, who I knew was Arsenio Galina. He was strapped to the chair with rope and now they were standing, eye to eye. Galina had swallowed hard more than once as he listened to me say more and more. Not only had I brought down Barker and his crew, but I had been forced to gather an entirely different story around Galina and his people, even the ones who had betrayed him right in front of his face.

He was listening to me lay out fact after fact that made perfect sense about the betrayals happening around him. I spoke as fast as I could. I wanted to save my own life, but I was hopeful my brother might be saved too. He was in terrible shape and all I could do was pray that God would have mercy on him, or that someone would have seen something when these men snatched me off of the street.

"Agh!" Galina howled, flipping over a chair after listening to me for long enough. His chest rose and fell like a wild animal's. "Bring him closer to me," he gritted. His men all looked at the other guy, the traitor, sympathetically.

"Boss . . . um . . . maybe you should calm—" the traitor started.

"Shut your fucking mouth!" Galina roared so loud that the man fell to his knees.

"What about the girl? And the other guy here?" another one of Galina's men asked.

"I am going to take care of them too. I haven't forgotten them," Galina said calmly now. They rushed around and took their positions, not knowing what move to make next. Galina stood in the middle of the floor for a few minutes. Then out of nowhere he started smashing shit, kicking over chairs and tables, and roaring loudly. He was a man possessed, and he was going to stop at nothing until he felt satisfied that everyone involved had suffered longer and much harder than he did.

"Please, boss, you have to believe me. This girl is lying," the traitor begged.

I watched through my swollen eyes and wished every single pain I felt on the man. I didn't care anymore; my heart had grown as cold as ice now.

"She's not lying! How would she know so much about the business?" Galina barked. He rushed over and slapped the man across his face so hard, blood and spit shot from her mouth.

"Agh! Please!" the traitor screamed. I'd taken hours of ass

whupping from Galina since he'd captured me. I smirked. I loved seeing someone else in pain. Even if Galina killed me after this, I felt I would die satisfied. I had officially broken up their entire criminal enterprise and turned them against one another. A job well done. And regardless if I died or not, I had still achieved my life goal of winning an Emmy Award.

"You were supposed to be like my brother. We came to this country together with big dreams and hopes. I was loyal to you from the day we got on this soil. You told me there was nothing you wouldn't do for me, and I told you the same. You fucking lied!" Galina spat.

The traitor hung his head and sobbed like a baby. "I wanted to be boss too! You never gave me a chance! You took everything for yourself. The women, the cars, the money—you took all the best! You took the most! I never wanted to live in your shadow! We were supposed to be partners and you never wanted anyone to get more than you!" the traitor screamed, finally confessing to his jealousy and betrayal.

As I stood there, I suddenly started to feel sorry for the traitor.

No! Fuck him! He did some disgusting things to me, I reminded myself.

"Kill him," Galina rasped. "Kill him!" His voice rose to a fever pitch. He wasn't giving up.

My hand shook now. I vowed I never wanted to witness another murder in my life after the ones I'd seen. But if I was going to die too, it didn't even matter anymore.

"Please, brother, don't do this. We both made mistakes. We are still family," the traitor cried.

"Kill him!" Galina screamed again.

His men rushed past me like a swarm or a SWAT team. Startled, I stumbled a little bit.

"Now!" he screamed at them.

"First tell me why you couldn't be a real brother. Why did you have to take everything for yourself?" the traitor spoke up, and asked him.

Galina looked at him pitifully. He shook his head from left to right.

"Kill him before I kill all of you," Galina whispered. He was trying to hold on to his composure. All of his men lifted their guns almost at the same time. They leveled the guns at the traitor. "Please! I'm begging—" the traitor started.

Bam! Bam! A barrage of bullets went off and silenced him. I knew then that he was dead.

I turned away, unable to watch and knowing that the wrath was about to be turned back to me. So many thoughts raced through my head about whether I was going to live or die. And if I was murdered, how exactly would my life end? This was no way to leave this earth.

"Tell me why you didn't just kill me weeks ago," I asked softly, tears running down my battered face.

"The same reason you didn't try to expose the rest of the story. Timing is everything and you, of all people, know that," Galina answered. "Everything in time and for a reason. You get what you deserve for the things you do in life. It's called karma," he was saying.

The next thing I heard was like a loud explosion. I dropped down and everyone began to scramble. When I looked up, what looked like a huge police tank was driving into the building.

"Get out of here!" Galina screamed, but it was too late. Within minutes there were police officers upon him and his men. I couldn't believe my eyes, ears, *or* my other senses. I was overjoyed and overwhelmed at the same time.

A police officer tackled Galina to the floor. "Ooof," he gagged as a fist slammed into his diaphragm, causing all of the wind in his body to blow hard out of his mouth. I watched as vomit spewed out of his mouth right after.

"Hit that bitch-ass nigga again!" a deep baritone voice commanded. With that, another sledgehammer-sized fist slammed into Galina's jaw. I saw the blood and spit shoot from between his lips. This shit was unreal.

Tears of joy drained down my face. The salt from the blood stung the open cuts on my split bottom lip. We were being saved.

"Is there anyone else in here hurt?" the deep voice asked me.

I nodded my head vigorously. "Yes, my brother. He is dying. Please try to save him."

As the gravity of the whole situation finally settled into my aching, bruised, and battered brain, I coughed and wheezed, trying to tell them what happened and where Kyle might be. I had been moved to two different rooms through this whole ordeal. Each raggedy breath hurt like hell. I knew then that some of my ribs had been shattered.

"Where is the body?" the voice boomed again. This time they forced Galina to stand up and face them.

"I'll ask you one more time, Arsenio Galina—where the fuck did you take her brother?" the head cop growled.

"Fuck you and her," Galina answered. My entire body went cold, like my veins had been injected with ice water. I knew right then that if he didn't tell them where Kyle was, time was going to run out. I knew at a minimum my brother had been shot and electrocuted. Although my heart was galloping, something told me to tell them to check out back in those vans. I knew Galina and his people were the types to bury someone to hide the evidence, even if he was still fighting for his life.

"Please! Please find my brother," I managed through battered lips. Each word was painful coming out, but I was a woman possessed at that moment, so I didn't feel a thing. Nothing at all, except fear for my brother's life. He was my twin. He was my life.

As they were taking him out, I heard Galina let out a raucous, maniacal laugh. "You won't find him in time. He is a dead man, and don't forget, you are a dead woman too. I never forget when people owe me debts," Galina spat as he was moved past me.

"It's pieces of shit like you that make my job worth it," one of the police officers hissed, and then dragged Galina out of the place.

The heat of anger that lit up my chest from his words was probably enough to make me kill him with my bare hands, if I could've. I bucked my body out of anger, but that just made shit worse.

"We found him!" I heard a police officer announce. "Let's get them all loaded into ambulances and get them out of here."

Just then, I saw my mother and Liza rushing toward me.

"Khloé! Oh, my God!" my mother bawled.

"Agh!" I cried, falling into her arms. Here she was again, saving my life. I didn't know how she always knew how to find us, and how she always felt when we were hurting or in trouble, but I was surely grateful for my mother's gift that day.

"Come on, let them get you into the ambulance," she said, letting go of my battered body. "Don't worry about Kyle. I will make sure . . ." She started to speak, but her voice trailed off. I knew that meant she didn't want to make me any promises, just in case my brother was dead.

"Agh!" I screamed out, and panted for breath at the same time, while they helped me into the back of the ambulance. The pain was unbearable. I could barely catch my breath. Small squirms of light flitted through my eyes. I was literally seeing stars from how bad I was hurting.

"Don't you worry. All of this won't be for nothing. It's far from over, and it won't all be for nothing," my mother told me as she closed the back of the ambulance doors.

I opened my battered and swollen eyes and stared up at the blinding light dangling from the ceiling inside the ambulance. I was praying and inviting death to just come take me away from this pain. I told God if my brother died, I never wanted to live another day. The EMTs saw that I was upset and agitated. They gave me a sedative, and before long I could feel the walls closing in on me. Before the darkness and the shock engulfed me, though, I thought about Kyle and all the shit we had done to get to this point. We were as thick as thieves. I had his back and he had mine. Now all of that had changed.

What am I going to do now?

18

THE VERDICT

In the name of my brother, I made sure that I was ready to give my testimony in the trials of Detective Keith, Anton Barker, Arsenio Galina, and several other members of their nasty organization. I had limped down the long aisle of the courtroom each time I was called into court, my leg messed up from the beatings I'd taken.

The last day I sat amongst the crowd. The courtroom was pin-drop quiet, although it was packed to capacity. The jury foreman stood up; the rustle of his suit made the inside of the room feel tense. He cleared his throat. The judge asked the foreman if the jury had reached the verdict. The foreman said yes and unfolded a piece of paper. He opened his mouth and the words seemed to come out in slow motion: "We, the jury, in the case of the *Commonwealth of Virginia* versus *Anton Barker,* find the defendant guilty of all of the charges against him, first-degree murder."

A loud round of groans and moans filtered around the room. "Order!" the judge screamed, banging his gavel. The foreman continued apprehensively. He could feel the evil eyes bearing down on him. "We, the jury, also find the defendant guilty of the charge of child endangerment," he finished up. The courtroom erupted in pandemonium. There were screams and moans. People were moving; reporters were running out of the courtroom so they could be the first to break the news.

I wasn't there in that capacity today. I wasn't worried about a news story or getting the best shot or camera angle. I was there to see all of my hard work really and truly pay off. I had learned it wasn't about the story. It was about justice: real justice in the name of those who weren't there to speak for themselves, like my brother. I swiped away the happy tears from my face and mouthed, "Thank you, Jesus." In my mind justice had finally been served.

I could hear the news reporters and tabloid media personalities screaming: "Mrs. Barker, your husband was just convicted of murder! The verdict has shocked the nation!"

I watched as Anton Barker's wife was ushered out of the courtroom, shrouded by the team of attorneys that had failed her husband. I smiled inside. I had done it. Anton Barker was a convicted man. Once we all hit the courthouse doors, the throngs of reporters moved in for the kill.

"Ms. Mercer! How did you do it? How did you put away so many murderers and stay alive?" reporters screamed as I tried to get out of the building. The other slew of reporters jammed their microphones in Mrs. Barker's face and asked her just as many questions. She kept her head hung low, hiding her face with her arms. She didn't want anyone to see the shame across her face. I felt a pang of sadness for her and her son, but then I thought about my brother and that feeling quickly faded away.

Now the replay of the courtroom scene almost brought a smile to my face again. I sat in the network studio and watched everything on the big screen. The network had chosen to use the scene as an opening for the piece they were doing on my life and my journey from junior reporter to Emmy winner to almost getting killed for a story. I chuckled as I heard the correspondent rehearsing her opening statements. I remembered my days of being nervous and rehearsing behind the scenes at the news station before a big on-air moment. I had really done it all and gotten to this point. I was so important that reporters wanted to interview me now, instead of the other way around. It was all fascinating, to say the least.

"Tonight, on *Nightline,* we bring you the story of Khloé Mercer. Once a beautiful, hungry, young junior reporter, she was charged with going out and finding a newsworthy story. She ended up finding that story, but also narrowly escaped losing her life to shed light on one of the biggest scandals to ever rock the state of Virginia. Tonight you will hear Ms. Mercer tell the story of how she went from a backroom junior reporter, who reported on petty robberies and car accidents, to the most popular reporter in Virginia, and equally the most hated woman in the whole state of Virginia. The police say she helped bring down a scandal in the Norfolk Police Department so huge that they had to fire nearly sixty percent of their police force for being corrupt. We will take you through Khloé's life, starting with her humble beginnings in the roughest neighborhood in Norfolk, through her struggles growing up without a father after he was murdered, and dealing with a mother who was drug addicted. We'll talk about her current life as an Emmy Award–winning news reporter who is now retired and has taken up writing a book about the Barker corruption case. Stay tuned as we bring you the story of Khloé Mercer, a woman who in her own account brought down the biggest, most corrupt government in the history of the United States."

I smirked to myself as I listened to my best friend, Liza,

the newest host of the television special that would feature my story, rehearse the opening for our interview. I chuckled just thinking about how far Liza and I had come from being screamed at by Christian to now being the interviewer and interviewee on a nationally recognized network show. It was nervous laughter, I have to admit, but I was thinking, *You damn right we are here!* We both deserved this moment. Period. And now the world would know the truth about my story.

I walked away from almost being killed. But my brother didn't. I folded my arms across my chest as I thought about the entire ordeal. I didn't care that people there were Barker supporters that still didn't believe my story; I knew the truth. I was going to tell it like it was, like it really happened. Not like the opposing-side media had made it out to be when everything first happened.

Liza finished her intro and was suddenly ready to get down to business with the interview. She smiled at me as she got into her chair directly across from me and they put the finishing touches on her makeup. I was so proud of Liza. I could feel the love from her and I knew she felt it from me too. It was clear that even Liza was now one of the number one news correspondents in Virginia, but she still thought of me as the best and as a mentor. She just didn't know how much I also looked up to her. I was old news in the business now, and she was new and improved. She had stepped up her game and worked hard, but the whole time she was there for me through my grieving and my recovery.

"Are you ready?" Liza asked, still flashing her beautiful, newly-paid-for smile. I inhaled deeply.

"As ready as I'm going to get," I answered, exhaling. I hadn't really talked about all of the intricacies of my story in one place. In fact, I had definitely pushed some things into the far reaches of my mind. Today, however, like I promised when the network agreed to pay me two hundred thousand for my story, I was going to tell everything—raw, uncut, and in their faces.

"Okay, Ms. Mercer, or do you prefer Khloé?" Liza stumbled over her words.

"Khloé is fine." I wanted to tell her it was me, not to be so nervous, but I knew I couldn't give her any advice while we were rolling.

"Khloé, you sit here as one of the most talked-about women in America. Many people say you literally risked life and limb for a news story. Although you say you didn't do it for the story, this couldn't be how you planned your life to be. I mean, you can't even walk down the street without someone recognizing you. You've received death threats, and you lost your brother as a casualty of bringing this very scandalous story to life," Liza stated, her open-ended question leading me down her little path.

"No, I definitely did not just do it for the story. As a little girl I always knew I would be famous, though. I also knew I'd be just as fabulous as I am today—" I began.

"But did you know you'd be famous at this cost?" Liza blurted out, cutting in before I could say anything else. Her words struck me like a gut punch. I didn't expect that. I grabbed the edges of the chair and gripped them tightly. I was more determined than ever to tell the story now. I opened my mouth and thought about how it had all gotten started. I needed people to know, and I needed Kyle to be remembered.

After my interview ended, I grabbed my things and headed out the side door of the station. Exiting this way made me less accessible to the media that was posted up across the street. While I was walking toward my car, I noticed there was a piece of paper placed between my windshield and the windshield wiper. Puzzled by the sudden appearance of it, I looked around my immediate surrounding to see if someone was watching me. But after a quick search, I saw nothing or no one. So I grabbed the note and slowly opened it.

I saw how you broke the Anton Barker's case wide open. So I need you to help me find out who murdered my husband. I believe that he was involved in a cover-up. I will pay you top dollar. Please call me at 555-0010.
—Anonymous